A DOCTOR
IN THE
HOUSE

A DOCTOR IN THE HOUSE

•

HELEN WINGO

AVALON BOOKS
THOMAS BOUREGY AND COMPANY, INC.
401 LAFAYETTE STREET
NEW YORK, NEW YORK 10003

PRINTED IN THE UNITED STATES OF AMERICA
ON ACID-FREE PAPER
BY HADDON CRAFTSMEN, SCRANTON, PENNSYLVANIA

For Dee, My Love
and
Mary, My Beloved Sister,
Who left too soon

Chapter One

Why today of all days?

Cari Masterson mentally railed at the eccentric electricity at Hawthorne House as she ripped off her bluebird-decorated T-shirt. No buzz of an alarm clock. No coffee.

Hanging the shirt haphazardly in her locker, she reached for a tunic, pulled it over her caramel-colored hair, exchanged decorative tennies for white clogs, and rushed out of the nurses' lounge. Greeting passing co-workers, she skidded to a stop before a huge scheduling board inside the surgery department. She scanned the list, locating her assigned room, and lifted an eyebrow. The procedure, an intermedullary rodding, was familiar, but the surgeon's name wasn't. She turned hurriedly to pick up a computer printout for the case. She was ten minutes behind schedule and she didn't need a new surgeon today. A second too late, she realized another board-scanner obstructed her path.

She gasped as a strong hand gripped her arm, realigning her center of balance. Embarrassed, she stared at the toe of a size-nine–plus sneaker protruding from beneath her size-six clog planted atop the victim's foot.

''Sorry,'' Cari mumbled breathlessly.

''No problem,'' a deep, amiable voice answered. ''I may need a walking cast for a few days. . . .''

Cari looked up to gaze into a pair of humorous green eyes, and for a moment she forgot she was ten minutes behind schedule and had to get off duty on time. She didn't know who moved first, he to drop his hands or she to remove her foot from his.

She stepped back. Before she had time to apologize further, a familiar voice boomed in her ear.

''Cari, you're late.'' Aware the foot victim was moving away, Cari turned toward the voice. An approaching nurse thrust forward a cup emitting the aroma of fresh-brewed coffee.

Accepting the cup, Cari spared a second to grin mischievously at her friend. ''No 'welcome back,' 'how was your spring vacation,' 'I missed you'?''

''Welcome back. How was your vacation? I missed you. . . . Will you take call for me tonight?'' Breathless, the nurse kept her gaze glued to Cari.

Laughter erupted from Cari's throat. ''It's not easy to refuse such an eloquent request, Reba.''

Reba beamed. ''I knew you wouldn't let me down.''

''Flattery plus bribery,'' Cari declared, nodding at the coffee cup as she finger-combed her short tresses, ''will get you almost anything this morning.''

Reba eyed her warily. ''Why do I hear 'almost' louder than any other word in that statement?''

Cari hesitated, taking a long sip of coffee before answering. ''Because I have to attend a Buena Vista City Council meeting this evening.''

Reba stared at Cari. ''Since when did you become civic minded?''

''Since someone started wanting to tear down Gran's old house.'' The explanation sounded terser than Cari intended.

Reba pursed her lips. ''I know how you feel about that Victorian relic, but couldn't you champion your cause at next week's council meeting?'' A dreamy look spread over Reba's features. ''I have a date with the most gorgeous male in the physical therapy department.''

Cari grimaced. She was usually amenable to changing call times, especially with Reba, who'd helped her ease into the operating room routines.

''I am sorry, Reba.'' Regret echoed in her voice. ''You know I'd trade if I could.''

Reba's drooped shoulders and woeful face touched Cari more than she would have admitted. But she had to be firm. The Victorian relic known as Hawthorne House represented the one stable summer, albeit short, in her unstable childhood. A childhood spent in hotel rooms, apartments, or seedy motels, depending on her mother's current financial and marital status.

''I'm sure someone will trade.'' She turned to continue her interrupted search for a computer printout for her case.

How could she expect Reba to understand her love for the aging Victorian structure? It wasn't easy to explain that beyond the weather-grayed siding and tilted front porch, she saw the love and acceptance her grandmother had shown in leaving an illegitimate grandchild half interest in the house. The gift meant roots and security and acknowledgment as a family member. A gift she would not give up easily.

She straightened her shoulders, unconsciously

checking her tunic pocket for scissors and pen, and flipped open the printout. Today's problem wasn't just another plumbing or electrical crisis. It was serious.

She raised her eyes from perusing the printed sheet at the sound of her supervisor's voice.

''Cari, glad you're back.'' The O.R. supervisor's voice rang with sincerity. ''I've scheduled you with the fractured femur. We have a new orthopedic surgeon on staff. Dr. Carson. Dr. Barstow is monitoring him. He's operating in your room today.'' She lifted her gaze at a call from the unit secretary and then hurried away.

Cari nodded to her superior's departing back, wondering with chagrin if she'd just walked over the newest staff member of Buena Vista Hospital.

Shelving the thought, she picked up a mask and hair cover, and rushed to open ''her'' room.

Placing an orthopedic pack on a waist-high steel table, she unfolded the outer cover and caught a glimpse of a figure in the doorway of the room. She finished removing the outer cover before she looked up to acknowledge the newcomer.

''Good morning.'' She blinked at the tall, now familiar, scrub-suited man.

''Good morning.'' He returned her greeting with no trace of animosity over their meeting at the scheduling board.

''Dr. Carson?''

His eyes focused on Cari in friendly appraisal. ''Guilty.''

''I'm Cari Masterson. I'm circulating for your case today.'' She wasn't sure how to phrase her next sentence. Did he expect another apology? Or did he want another circulating nurse? She decided his friendly demeanor might tolerate a nonserious approach. "That is, if you're able to stand after I tromped on your foot."

He chuckled, to her relief. "I don't qualify for sick leave, so I guess I'll have to grin and bear the pain."

Cari laughed nervously. "I could apply ice packs to your foot while you're operating."

"I imagine you'll be busy enough without adding any extra duties," the surgeon said amiably. He leaned against the side of the door. "I thought I might check with you on the instruments for the intermedullary rodding."

Cari nodded, a professional face erasing the brief trepidation. "I have the large ortho tray, a maxi driver, k wires, guide pins . . ." Cari paused, trying to recall the instruments listed on Dr. Carson's card.

"Efficient." Admiration tinged his voice.

"I can't take credit." The irrepressible smile building beneath Cari's mask radiated to her eyes. "I have a cheat card—that is someone filled in a card showing your preference of instruments and sutures and other supplies, and I just followed instructions."

Dr. Carson raised an eyebrow. "A self-deprecating twentieth-century Florence Nightingale?"

Cari laughed. "Just honest." She walked to a counter to pick up the physician's card and strode to the doorway, extending the card to the physician. "Maybe you'd like to check the list."

The surgeon accepted the card, perused it quickly, and returned it to Cari. "Looks good." He remained standing in the doorway.

Cari slid the card in her pocket, wishing the tall

surgeon with the humorous eyes would go check his patient or something. ''Is there anything else I can help you with, Dr. Carson?'' she said at last.

''Now that you mention it,'' the surgeon drawled, ''there is. I've been staying with Jim Barstow and his wife for the last few days, and it's time I found a place of my own. One of the nurses mentioned a vacancy in the house where you live.''

Cari laughed briefly and walked back to pick up an instrument pack. ''This nurse didn't suggest you rent in the house where I live, did she?''

Dr. Carson echoed Cari's laughter. ''No. I think she said something like how happy she was to move.''

''The apartment she's so glad to leave is two rooms converted into a living room, mini-kitchen, and bedroom.''

''What more does a bachelor need?''

''It's not posh.'' Cari unwrapped the outer cover of the instruments. Why did she downplay the assets of Hawthorne House at a time like this? A vacant apartment didn't bring in any money. She turned to look at the doctor, her sense of fairness overriding her financial problems. ''To be honest, the building needs a new roof, not to mention a number of repairs under that roof.''

''If I remember Buena Vista, the rainy season is almost over.'' His lips curved in a generous grin. ''Is that all?''

''The apartments on the second floor share a bathroom''—she paused for emphasis—''with a temperamental shower.''

''If it has indoor plumbing, it's one up on my last

residence. Anything else?'' The surgeon's tone was droll.

The fleeting memory of the water in the basement that had kept the resident handyman up most of the night struggled to surface. Cari ignored it. Flooding wouldn't strike twice in the same place. She selected another sterile pack before her conscience interceded. ''It's not where an up-and-coming surgeon would live.''

''Do I look like a snob?'' The doctor's eyebrows lifted charmingly.

''I didn't mean to imply you were.'' Cari busied her eyes and hands with opening the pack. He looked like a tall, handsome, amiable hunk. Tresses of nut brown hair escaped the paper cap covering his well-shaped head. A high forehead and wide-set eyes blended well with a shapely nose, full, generous lips, and the hint of deep smile lines in his cheeks. His demeanor was by no means aloof. Cari lowered the contents of her package to the sterile table. Living next door to the doctor couldn't be all bad—if one didn't become too friendly. And a doctor in the house was better than a handyman if you had a midnight attack of gastritis. She took a calming breath. ''I just meant there are nicer places in Buena Vista.''

''Where are these nicer places you think suitable for this hopefully 'up-and-coming' surgeon?''

Cari relinquished the thought of a resident doctor at Hawthorne House. ''On the south side. Condominiums to die for, I hear.''

''With a rental fee fit to precipitate a heart attack in a financially strapped surgeon.''

Cari hid her grin behind her mask. Dr. Randolph

Carson was not the stereotypical new surgeon. The last one on staff, she recalled, had flaunted his potential income via a flashy sports car and a house with an indoor swimming pool and more bathrooms than Buena Vista's one hotel.

She turned back to the doctor. ''If it's bargain-basement prices you're looking for, Hawthorne House is the place to go.'' Unusually glad to see the surgical tech entering the room, she introduced the young woman to the doctor. Then she glanced at the clock on the wall with more of a show than necessary. ''Time for me to get your patient.''

She hurried from the room. She'd tried to dissuade him, hadn't she? What more could a respectable conscience ask?

She strode toward the holding area and paused at the sound of her name.

''Hi, Cari, looks like you got a little sun.'' The nurse pulled on a paper cap. ''Go someplace exciting?''

''Drove to San Francisco for the weekend, but most of the time I stayed at home painting and pounding nails—and straining muscles I didn't know I had.''

The other nurse grinned before donning a mask. ''That's why my husband is a confirmed renter. He wants to vacation in Tahiti next year.''

''Sounds like paradise,'' Cari said. Her heart wasn't in her words. Paradise for her was saving Hawthorne House from a wrecking crew. She glanced toward the double lines deterring nonsurgical personnel from entering the operating area, to see a hospital bed, complete with a small boy in leg traction, roll to a stop.

''I see my patient is here.'' Cari nodded at the nurse and walked briskly to the holding area.

Greeting the transportation aide, she accepted the patient chart and stepped to the bed.

''Kevin.'' She spoke in a friendly tone to the traction-tethered child. ''Looks like something happened to your leg.''

The boy turned toward her with a faint smile. ''That dumb skateboard didn't go where it was supposed to.'' Kevin's complaint sounded groggy. ''But the doctor said I'd be okay.''

''Doctors know those things,'' Cari said agreeably.

She opened the chart, scanned the results of the lab work, made a mental note to obtain X rays of the fractured femur, and checked for the physical exam report. She found it, complete with the doctor's signature—Randolph Carson. She grinned, flipping through the paperwork. He was not only handsome and amiable, he could write legibly. She let the grin slide. She wasn't looking for a handsome, amiable, legible writer this morning. Just a surgeon who started on time and kept on schedule. She wanted nothing to go wrong—she needed to get off duty on time. Closing the chart, she looked for an aide to help her push the bed along the inner corridor.

Cari halted the bed at the door of the fourth room, scanning inside for obstacles. Rolling the hospital bed into a room designed for a narrow table and equally narrow gurney was akin to driving a bus down a supermarket aisle. She signaled her helper and maneuvered the cumbersome carrier past the anesthesiologist's equipment.

"I'll be in to help move the patient in a minute," a deep, familiar voice called from the scrub room.

Cari's reply was automatic. "Thanks." Moving traction patients usually required two people to lift feet, two others at midbody, and the anesthesiologist to move the patient's head. Available OR personnel responded readily, and today she welcomed all the help she could get. Ignoring a twinge of pain from her back, Cari helped position the bed beside the narrow steel table and caught Kevin's glazed, insecure look.

She took his hand, caressing it soothingly as she checked the flow in the intravenous line attached to the young patient's arm. Aware another person had entered the room, she released Kevin's hand and glanced up to see the tall, scrub-suited man move across from her. Above his mask, the sea green eyes focused on her with a friendly gaze before he turned his attention to the young patient.

"Hi, Kev. Time to fix the leg, huh? I'm ready if you are."

Kevin turned his head a fraction, a near smile brightening his youthful face. "You remember about the skateboard contest?"

"How could I forget? You've reminded me twice a day for the last five days."

"Oh." Kevin's voice fell.

"Which is good," the masked man added. "I wouldn't want to miss the performance of my star patient."

"It's not 'til summer," Kevin said. "So I'll have time to practice, won't I?" His concern pushed through his drowsiness.

"The quicker we start, the sooner you'll be able to

begin practice. We need to move you from this bed first.''

''Do you have to?'' Kevin mumbled.

''I find bending over to operate puts a crease in my back, so I prefer you on a bed the nurses can raise. Okay?''

The gentle, humorous voice directed at the eleven-year-old touched Cari. She glanced at the surgeon, and the almost liquid tenderness in his eyes prompted an unusual wave of warmth somewhere in her chest.

The boy moaned, and the surgeon glanced toward the end of the bed. ''Not yet.'' He spoke calmly, stilling the hands of the aide who'd touched Kevin's fractured leg in preparation for the transfer from bed to operating table. The doctor's gaze swung toward the head of the bed where the anesthetist stood.

Syringe poised above the intravenous line, the anesthetist's gaze met the surgeon's eyes. ''I'll give him Versed. It's like a short-acting Valium. . . . He won't remember this.''

The orthopedic surgeon nodded in acknowledgment.

Without warning, Kevin flailed one hand outward, and both Cari and the surgeon reached to calm him. Only when the child relaxed as the medication took effect, did Cari become aware that her hands sandwiching Kevin's small fingers had been covered by the surgeon's large masculine one. Tanned, long, tapered fingers with short, manicured nails rested casually on her hand.

Feeling the surgeon's gaze, she looked up and a momentary wave of confusion touched her. She lowered her eyelids, acutely aware of her haphazardly filed nails and skin roughened by paint thinner. Certainly not the type of hands men longed to hold on dates. She resisted the urge to slide her fingers from their sandwiched position, grateful Dr. Carson couldn't see the blister on her palm.

She shook herself mentally. Why should she care what he thought of her less-than-soft skin and unprofessional manicure? The last thing she wanted was to become emotionally involved with a man—any man. A breath of relief filtered through her lungs when the anesthesiologist signaled the team to move the patient and the surgeon removed his hand.

The move to the operating table completed, Cari fastened safety straps around the patient, aware of the masked orthopedic surgeon striding back to the scrub room. Handing sutures, needles, and last-minute supplies to the scrub tech, she took a calming breath. She was always tense the first time she worked with a new surgeon. That didn't help as she prepped Kevin's injured leg. But the flutter in her chest was different from the nervousness she felt when working with a different doctor.

Moving away from the table, Cari involuntarily turned her head to gaze through the window to the scrub room. As if on cue, Randolph Carson's gaze met hers, sending a shock through her. Somehow, his look threatened to penetrate not only the layers of gauze, but Cari's carefully tended professional reserve.

Startled, Cari swung her gaze back to the operating table, focusing on the anesthesiologist as he visually checked the drip of fluid in the plastic chamber of the intravenous line before his gaze returned to the screen to check the changing numbers and fluctuating lines indicating the vital signs of the patient on the table.

His relaxed look calmed Cari. She glanced at the clock on the wall.

To her amazement, the case was on schedule. The momentary eye contact with Dr. Carson had seemed like an era. Professional aplomb slightly off balance, she turned to greet a doctor entering the room.

"Good morning." The voice of Dr. Barstow boomed across the busy room, steadying Cari with its familiarity.

He turned toward Cari as the new member of the staff stepped into the room. "I think everyone has met Dr. Carson except you, Cari." He looked at the taller man. "Rand, this is Cari Masterson. Don't try to get away with any shortcuts when she's in the operating room." He winked at Cari.

"I have met Cari," Rand Carson said. "And believe me, I wouldn't try to get away with scrubbing less than the full time." He held up his wet hands. "See?"

Cari lifted her eyes, her breath catching in her throat, and again felt a tremor of unrest. For no logical reason, she told herself. The eyes sparkling at her above the surgical mask held nothing but goodwill. Cari released her imprisoned breath, letting the professional smile beneath the mask touch her eyes.

"You look reliable," she said with a hint of humor.

"Not to mention Dr. Barstow stood beside me all the time I scrubbed." The new staff member turned from Cari to accept a towel from a scrub technician.

"How do you like Buena Vista?" the tech asked.

"Even better than the last time I was here. It seems I returned during the best weather."

"Spring is beautiful in northern California," she replied.

"Dr. Carson did his residency here a few years ago," Dr. Barstow explained to the room at large. "I, for one, am delighted to see him back."

"I think we all are," the scrub tech said with enthusiasm. Her look lingered on the surgeon as she opened a gown for him.

Cari cast a baleful look at the tech. The last thing she needed today was a groupie, especially for a new surgeon. With luck, and lack of an adoring fan club, he might remain tolerable.

Which could be more difficult for him than some. Rand Carson was even better looking than the actor whose name he shared. His eyes sparkled warmly above the mask as he acknowledged the scrub tech and discarded the towel used to dry his dripping fingers. He extended his arms for a sterile gown, and Cari noted his deeply tanned arms. A wry smile twitched at the lips beneath her mask. Catch him painting an age-scarred house or pounding nails into timeworn porch steps. Golf or tennis at some country club, more likely, kept him in great shape. Involuntarily, she noticed that great shape had the blue scrub trousers stopping an inch short of his ankles and the matching tunic straining to cover his muscular shoulders. Irritated at her momentary assessment, she retreated to the suture shelf, puzzled at her lapse of professionalism.

When she turned, the scrub nurse was holding a sterile glove for the orthopedic surgeon as she gazed at him with widened eyes. "I hope you'll stay this time, Dr. Carson."

"Oh, he's here to stay," Dr. Barstow interjected.

''Dr. Carson left to do a tour of duty overseas after he finished his residency. But he's back just as we planned. We're going into practice together.''

Dr. Carson moved to the table to assist with draping the patient. ''I'm glad to be home.''

Eyes bright with enthusiasm, Dr. Barstow extended his arms for a gown. ''We have great plans for the medical care of Buena Vista residents.''

Cari smiled at Dr. Barstow's ardor, looking at him with interest. But the anesthetist's voice interrupted any further vocalization from Dr. Barstow. He and the new specialist stepped to the table. Only then did Cari lift her eyes to Dr. Carson's face. His glance touched hers, solemn, professional, and impersonal. Then he looked down at the injured leg and accepted a scalpel from the scrub tech.

Between her duties, Cari watched the surgeon work smoothly and efficiently, keeping her thoughts on a professional basis. Finishing the operation, he stayed to assist with the bandages. Retrieving a roll of tape, Cari removed the scissors from her pocket and snipped the adhesive evenly before she handed the surgeon the strip.

Securing the bandage, Dr. Carson dipped his head toward the pocket of her tunic. ''Are you always prepared for any emergency?''

Cari laughed shakily. ''Once a Girl Scout, you know . . .'' She moved away quickly to assist with the unconscious patient, feeling a sting of guilt. She'd never lived in one place long enough to belong to a Girl Scout troop. She'd never lived in one place long enough to belong. . . .

To her relief, Dr. Barstow spoke to his peer, and

the two surgeons walked toward the door in conversation. Banishing her momentary lapse from professionalism, Cari glanced at the clock. The case had finished on schedule.

Nothing had gone wrong.

So why did she feel so unnerved?

Chapter Two

Jim Barstow removed his gown, crushed it into a blue paper ball, and tossed it into a roll-away trash bag. "I have a problem with our appointment this evening," he said to Rand. He motioned for his friend to precede him from the operating room. "My in-laws are arriving in San Francisco on an evening flight. We're driving in to pick them up."

Rand smiled with a mixture of teasing and benevolence. "The prospective grandparents must be getting restless." He pulled the paper cover from his hair and glanced back at the surgical scene. He was pleased with the surgery. He would have preferred to stay a few moments with his patient, though he knew the child would be in the capable hands of the anesthesiologist until he was released to the recovery room nurse. He would have liked to thank the efficient circulating nurse. But after loosening his gown, she'd quickly moved away to assist the anesthetist. He would have waited until she was free, but Jim had looked at him expectantly. A twinge of disappointment touched him as his colleague almost propelled him through the doorway. Perhaps he could catch Cari Masterson later. He might even suggest she help on more of his cases.

* * *

Clearing the room after the last case, Cari walked to the supply room and found Reba checking instruments. She tugged her mask down. "Did you find someone to take call?" Her voice echoed her concern.

"No problem. Sharleen is willing."

Cari nodded in relief. "You know I'd trade if it wasn't for the zoning change item on the council agenda."

"Wouldn't it be easier to talk your aunt into keeping the place?" Reba pulled a sterile pack from the shelf.

"I've tried. She lives in Alaska, doesn't know me, and may not want to. Her return letters were polite, vague, and indifferent to the future of Hawthorne House."

Reba moved to another shelf. "So what's the rush about the zoning change?"

"Last month, a cousin and her husband showed up saying the house needs more repairs than my aunt can afford. It seems my aunt has just gone through a divorce. My cousin is concerned with protecting her mother's interests. She said my aunt wants to sell."

"So why aren't you delighted? I believe I recall you complaining after we finished a case at three o'clock one morning that you felt you were working to support a house."

Cari sighed. "It had been a long night."

"You've forgotten about spending every spare penny on supplies and every free minute on repairs, when, as you railed, no one else cares?"

"I've come to terms with my aunt's refusal to pour money down the drain." Cari plopped a lap pack on a cart. "Though, I'll admit, even taking as much call time as possible, the money won't stretch to cover everything that's needed."

"Call your aunt. Plead your case."

"Why would she listen? I can't imagine she was pleased to find I'd received a share of her legacy."

"You won't know unless you talk to her." Reba placed another instrument aside. "How did the intermedullary rodding go with the new guy?"

"Good." Cari shook her head. The thought of Dr. Randolph Carson that Cari had kept at bay all afternoon returned. "Good," she repeated.

"I worked with him on one case." Reba sighed heavily. "If I didn't have a positively absorbing interest in a certain physical therapist, I'd take call forever to be assigned to his operating room on a permanent basis."

Cari shook her head. "You said the same thing about Dr. Kelsey two months ago."

Reba rolled her eyes. "He was nice," she said nostalgically. "He was also truthful. He told me he was engaged to a medical student in New York."

"And you never brightened his door again."

"My aim is marriage, not mistress," Reba said humorously.

Cari grinned. "I wish you well."

Reba paused, one hand on a wrapped package. "If I can't chase Dr. Carson, the next best thing I can hope for is that you will."

"Don't start," Cari warned teasingly.

"What have you got against marriage?"

"It's what marriage has against me that counts. I don't think anyone in my family line can sustain a lasting relationship. My maternal grandparents are divorced. Counting my parents' brief live-in arrangement, my mother has had four failed relationships, and her current marriage is about as stable as a brick shed standing on the San Andreas Fault. On the other side of the family, my uncle is a bachelor and my aunt has just gotten a divorce.'' She plucked another package from a shelf and sighed. ''Happy-ever-after endings only happen in fairy tales.''

''Someday the right man will come along and bowl you over when you aren't looking,'' Reba said cheerfully.

''Not if I can help it.'' Cari rolled her eyes, finished selecting her supplies, and rolled the cart toward the door. ''I'm gonna dash upstairs for a sec to see Delia and Kevin.'' She wiggled two fingers at her friend. ''Don't stay out too late.''

''Yes, mother,'' Reba giggled.

Leaving the cart in the operating room suite, Cari covered her scrub suit with an oversize gown and left the surgical area. Minutes later, she entered a patient room, stopping abruptly at the sight of the tall, genial surgeon standing beside Kevin's bed. The navy blue blazer and gray slacks he wore fitted him far better than the OR scrub suit.

''I came to see Kevin's mother,'' she explained somewhat breathlessly.

He smiled. ''Is it routine for a member of the nursing team to visit relatives of the patient?''

Cari clutched a slipping sleeve on the oversize gown. ''Kevin's mother and I worked together on the evening shift when I first came to the hospital.''

He nodded, glancing at the sleeping child. ''The

floor nurse said Mrs. Sharpe went to the dining room for coffee. I thought I'd wait here a few minutes and talk to her. Join me.''

Cari pushed the opposite sleeve of the gown up her arm until the cuff reached her elbow. In the brief moment following the orthopedic surgeon's departure from the operating room earlier, she'd entertained the thought of looking drop-dead gorgeous in a figure-hugging dress the next time she met him. With manicured nails! But here she stood in a gown sliding toward her unkempt nails and billowing to her ankles. She hadn't even applied lipstick when she'd removed her mask.

Unease hurried her reply. ''Thanks, but I have only a minute. I'll catch Delia another time.'' She hesitated, sensing the abruptness of her words, but her vocabulary suddenly seemed as empty as a new computer disk. Raising a hand in departure, she left the room as briskly as she'd entered it, not slowing until she was on the staircase leading to the OR.

She scowled at the cream-colored walls lining the steps. What was her problem?

He was just another surgeon. Which made him even less of a candidate for a successful relationship, in her opinion. Doctors spent long hours at the office and the hospital, and from what she could see, patients had priority over family. She did concede their absences were probably no worse than those of her many stepfathers. In fact, they were probably better. The men her mother married were musicians and stand-up comics whose work kept her mother constantly packing suitcases.

She pushed the button to open the surgery entry

with more force than necessary and strode through the opening doors. She had enough problems. Thinking of the handsome, amiable Dr. Carson in any way except professionally was out of the question.

Entering the surgery department, she peeled off the voluminous gown and glanced at the clock on the wall. She would get off duty on time. Barring an accident en route, she would be at the council meeting to support her neighbor.

At a quarter to seven, Cari stood at the rear of the council chambers, scanning the front rows for a vacant chair, and frowned. Bypassing the warm shower, as she'd bypassed dinner, would have been wiser in order to arrive earlier.

Her irritation waned as she caught sight of the alert, friendly eyes of her elderly neighbor. Ben McGrath dropped one wrinkled eyelid and grinned. Cari lifted a thumb and held it up briefly, her spirits rising as she moved toward the empty chairs in the last row.

The oblong room, paneled in rich, dark wood, had double doors opening on one side and tall, glass-paned windows on the other. Cari selected a seat near a window.

Glancing to the front of the room again, she took in the raised platform. Bright overhead lights gleamed on the polished mahogany table in front of the three men and two women seated behind it. An auburn-haired councilwoman bent her head, listening to the man next to her, and laughed loudly. For some reason, it irritated Cari.

She curved her lips wryly. *Come on—lighten up!* Not everyone saw this gathering as a court of doom.

Mr. McGrath might make his point with someone sitting at that table.

She pulled her eyes away from the council members, peering past the open, slatted blinds and through the window. A line of cars waited at the stop sign while pedestrians moved in varied but confident gaits across the painted crosswalk. A group of four veered right, strolling toward the small restaurant on the corner. Nearer, children played gleefully on the grass under the benevolent, watchful eye of a mother sitting on a green bus bench. No one else appeared to be as tense as a gladiator primed to enter the arena. Cari closed her eyes briefly, took a sobering breath, and told herself to relax. The plea was like telling a snowflake to chill out in July.

She moved her gaze to the right, concentrating on the shimmering strands of water reaching high in the air to capture the fading rays of the sun. Following the fall of the droplets into the Spanish-style fountain, she saw a tall, familiar figure walk briskly past the fountain. A feather brushed the walls of her rib cage. He wore the same sports coat and trousers he'd had on earlier, but he'd changed to gym shoes. Out for an early evening walk to familiarize himself with his adopted city, she surmised. Almost before the thought was complete, the surgeon glanced toward the council chambers, then strode purposefully down the walkway to the entry.

The feather tickled her again, and Cari carefully averted her gaze before Rand Carson entered the double doors.

Acknowledging the pulsing awareness of his presence, she resisted the urge to see where he was sitting and forced herself to concentrate on the proceedings. She moved one short, clear-lacquered fingernail down the printed agenda and found the zoning change item third on the list.

As if she'd accomplished one mission and put it on pause, her subconscious pressed a key, letting thoughts of the handsome surgeon flood the screen of her mind.

She glanced around quickly, unable to do less than admire a man who'd worked all day, and possibly the night before, and still took time to attend a council meeting to acquaint himself with the community. His hair seemed lighter now, a pecan shade of brown, gilded by the lowering sun. In profile, his nose had a slight slant, as if it had been broken sometime, but his jaw was firm and void of any five o'clock shadow. She wondered if the lines radiating from his eyes were more noticeable in the glare of the overhead light—or was it that his smile at the occupant of the next chair increased the squint lines? A fleeting wish to be the recipient of that smile touched her, followed by an equally fleeting wish that happy-ever-after endings weren't only fairy-tale fiction.

She forced her thoughts back to the speaker. Her grandmother had been proud of her civic involvement and had tried, in their short time together, to instill the same feeling of responsibility in Cari. Yet, this was the first council meeting she'd attended since she'd moved to Buena Vista. And it was totally self-serving. If she had a choice she'd be watching a Western and sipping an after-dinner cup of coffee. But she'd missed the planning commission meetings when the zoning change had been discussed, so making points at this meeting was imperative.

The thought of the cup of coffee reminded her of the cream-cheese-and-jam sandwich she'd left, forgotten and untouched, on her kitchen counter. She glanced toward the restaurant, rejecting an earlier resolution to eat healthier, and placated the empty feeling in her stomach with a promise to pick up fries after the meeting. Involuntarily, she wondered if the friendly physician liked French fries.

The sound of a voice on the speaker system made her jerk her head back to the front of the room. The first two speakers were unfamiliar, and Cari listened inattentively until Mr. McGrath approached the podium with a slow, arthritic gait. Squinting, she concentrated on his thin figure as he reached for the microphone. She mustn't miss one word of her reason for being in the City Council chamber room.

Mr. McGrath spoke briefly, his gruff tone voicing his concern at the zoning change. He mentioned the increased traffic, the added fuel fumes that would damage his rose garden, and the desire to keep his peaceful neighborhood intact. Even to Cari, his plea wasn't powerful. Progress had already reached relentlessly within four blocks of their corner.

She swallowed, eyeing the well-dressed man who claimed the microphone next. She missed his name, but Ben had labeled him the speculator who'd bought two houses next to Hawthorne House with a view to selling. He'd added the man had an attorney prepared to address the zoning change.

She breathed a sigh of relief when the ''speculator'' left the podium. He'd been less positive than Ben, apologizing for his attorney's absence and pausing to fix a piercing gaze on the immobile chamber doors before he reluctantly relinquished the microphone to the next speaker on the agenda.

Cari clenched her fists. The zoning change for Hawthorne House and the other houses along the block was on hold, but any minute the professional pleader could burst through the double doors and charm the council members with his calculated rhetoric. What chance did a minor shareholder in Hawthorne House have to save the structure from demolition?

Shifting an intense gaze to the doors on her left, Cari barely listened to the Historical Society member claiming the microphone. He spoke in a deep, modulated tone, voicing a well-crafted speech in opposition to a proposed street name change.

''I realize,'' he continued, ''that the Historical Society has the ability to delay demolition on buildings of possible historical value, and that our members can only make a recommendation on this item.'' He paused, hoping to alert the audience with the momentary silence. ''But we want to voice our concern.''

Cari turned her head toward the speaker. What had he said about the membership of his group delaying the demolition of buildings with historical significance? She sat up straighter, focusing her attention on the man at the podium. To her dismay, the speaker beamed at the audience, waved the chubby, black wand in his hand as if to bless the congregation, and dramatically presented the microphone to the approaching speaker.

A dark-suited, well-groomed man accepted the microphone confidently and introduced himself as the attorney concerned with the zoning change. Cari's distress at the departure of the Historical Society member dwindled under the icy pressure building in her chest.

She leaned forward, holding her breath for fear of missing a word uttered into the microphone. The attorney politely but boldly explained his tardiness, the result of an accident on the freeway. He paused, peering at the council members, and a faint scowl touched his features. Cari followed his gaze and saw the mayor holding up one hand, palm outward.

It took a few minutes for Cari to realize the attorney's oratory had been placed on hold.

The mayor leaned toward the microphone. In an equally polite, even tone, he expressed regrets regarding the attorney's problem. ''But you did miss your time and the meeting must proceed according to protocol,'' he added firmly.

Cari heard an exclamation of irritation from the speculator, and a murmur of unrest a few seats away. She heard a reference to the item being tabled until the next council meeting in two weeks. Releasing her imprisoned breath, she turned her head toward the window, as if to draw a semblance of strength from the calmer scene outside. In the background, the whisper of voices abated.

She doubted if two weeks was enough time for her precious house to be declared an historic building, but in two weeks she might convince her relatives to keep the old house because of some historical value. Or sell it to someone who wouldn't tear it down.

Returning her gaze to the room, she saw the Historical Society member and his supporters rise and slip quietly down the aisle as the next speaker approached the podium. She stood and made her way toward the door to follow them.

The group separated as she reached the walk, heading in different directions. The speaker loped across the lawn to a waiting car driven by a young woman with a radiant smile. Cari stopped in midstride, her shoulders slumping. She doubted if the eloquent speaker voicing his interest in civic affairs a few moments earlier would welcome any new questions at this time.

She paused, catching her breath and her tumbling thoughts. Ben might not have been convincing on the zoning change subject, but then, the attorney hadn't even spoken. That must be a plus on their side. She glanced back toward the council room, wondering if Ben, too, would leave now. Perhaps she should wait a few moments.

When he didn't appear, she shifted her shoulder bag and started along the walk. She'd gone less than five feet when she heard her name.

Even before she turned, she knew the voice did not belong to Ben McGrath. Anxious as she was to hear her neighbor's assessment of the meeting, she wasn't disappointed to see Rand Carson. Nor could she suppress the rise of excitement as he approached.

From the sparkle in his eyes, he wasn't unhappy to see her either.

"Do nurses ordinarily attend council meetings?"

"No more often than surgeons, I would imagine." She grinned in welcome, sure that her own eyes were brighter than she would have wished. She didn't want him to see her as one of the groupies. "I came to hear a neighbor speak on a subject in which we share an interest. How about you?''

''I was supposed to meet Jim here, but he couldn't make it. He went to pick up his in-laws at the airport.''

''Dr. Barstow is interested in council meetings?''

''Only a zoning change item on the agenda.''

Cari's heart lurched. ''Oh.'' One word was all she could manage. She fumbled in the side pocket of her shoulder bag for the keys to her ten-year-old Ford. Dr. Barstow couldn't be the prospective purchaser of Hawthorne House! Not her favorite surgeon!

''The matter was postponed. Seems the attorney for the zoning change was delayed due to a freeway accident.''

Cari's heart dribbled downward, leaving a shaky feeling in her knees. The attorney for the zoning change involving the houses on the block including Hawthorne House was delayed due to a freeway accident!

''Jim should be able to attend the next meeting,'' the doctor continued cheerfully.

Cari glanced at the man strolling beside her. Nothing on his handsome face indicated any personal concern about the delayed attorney. Yet, Dr. Barstow had mentioned going into practice with him. Was that partnership based on building medical offices on the site of Hawthorne House and its neighboring structures? Tendrils of unrest moved in Cari's chest. Didn't she have enough on her plate without enemies in the workplace?

She saw the crosswalk ahead and quickened her step, anxious to part with the doctor before her tongue damaged her position in the operating room. Which in

the long run could diminish the finances to repair
Hawthorne House. She barely glanced at the surgeon,
murmured, ''See you in the OR,'' and stepped off the
curb.

The feel of his hand on her arm jolted her. She
looked up to see Dr. Carson indicating the red light
glaring at her across the crosswalk.

Cari grinned sheepishly. ''I wasn't even trying to
beat the crowd.'' She nodded toward the group of people entering the restaurant across the street.

''You missed lunch too?'' Rand cupped her elbow
as the light changed and they stepped onto the crosswalk.

''I had a salad between cases. But I hurried back to
be sure I got off duty on time.''

''And did you?''

''For a change.'' Cari stepped on the curb. ''Thanks
for saving me from a broken leg or something.''

''Couldn't have one of our operating room nurses
laid up in traction.''

''Thank you again.'' She turned to go into the restaurant. The doctor strode past her and held the door
open.

''I missed lunch altogether,'' he said cheerfully.

Before Cari could blink, a hostess appeared.
''Two?''

Rand Carson looked at Cari and raised an eyebrow.
''Two?''

Cari nodded. She wanted to be alone. She wanted
time to consider the new problem that had just cropped
up. She wanted to tell herself Rand Carson wasn't a
prospective buyer. And if he was, she had to set up

battle lines. How could she do that with him sitting across from her with a smile that would distract a nun?

The restaurant was brightly lit and furnished with booths of faux-oak tabletops and peach vinyl-covered seats. Potted philodendron, ficus, and trailing ivy plants decorated ledges on each wall. Leading them to an unoccupied booth, the middle-aged hostess distributed the oversize menus and smiled at Cari's companion as she parroted a list of specials for the day. Cari moved her gaze to the carnation preening amid a cluster of leather fern in the center of the table. She had to shelve her concern for Hawthorne House and make food her priority if she was going to get through the next hour.

''The hamburger with green chilies sounds good,'' the doctor said, laying the menu aside.

''I think I'd like that, Dr. Carson.''

''I could respond with Miss Masterson all evening, but I think Cari and Rand sounds friendlier.''

Cari laughed. ''Agreed.'' She was still grinning when the waitress took their order, and she echoed Rand's selection of iced tea instead of her usual cola.

Rand looked at her amiably. ''You're good in the operating room. You must like it.''

''I do.'' Hawthorne House slipped below the surface of her mind, replaced by her second passion.

''How long have you been at the medical center?''

''A little over a year.'' She touched one feathery edge of the carnation. ''But I've only been in the OR for six months.''

''I would have guessed longer. You're very efficient.'' Sea green eyes gazed at her admiringly.

''I was working in the operating room in Los Angeles when I learned my grandmother had cancer. I moved to Buena Vista to be near her.''

''Do you live with her?''

''She died eight months ago.''

''I'm sorry.''

Cari nodded in acknowledgment. ''Thank you.'' She gazed at the lacy carnation. ''I live in her house.''

''I thought you lived in an apartment.''

''I do. When I came back to Buena Vista, Gran was in a convalescent home and her house had been made into apartments.''

''Sounds nice.''

''I like it.'' Her voice sounded husky.

Gray green eyes, as calm as a tranquil sea, gazed into hers with that surprising liquid tenderness she'd seen before. ''Old houses hold memories.''

He paused as a young waitress stopped beside the table to place a tall glass of tea in front of Cari. When the waitress had moved on, he looked at Cari again. ''I called the 'dream condominiums' office just before I left for the council meeting. The office manager was vague about a date he could expect a vacancy. Is the vacancy sign still out where you live?''

The waitress approached again, and Cari waited for her to serve the aromatic burgers and leave. ''As far as I know. Mr. Branson, the resident manager, said it might cost more to fix the apartment up than it would bring in rent. Especially for a limited time.''

''Limited time?''

Cari glanced at him. Maybe he didn't know the zoning change concerned the house where she lived. ''The house may be sold.''

''Managers hate empty apartments.'' Rand turned

over one oval layer of the hamburger bun and spread a dollop of red sauce over the varied contents. ''Even if the place is up for sale.''

Involuntarily, Cari searched his face for any sign of guile, but Rand's eyes focused on the sandwich as he concentrated on adding spices and sauces as seriously as a chef on a cooking show. For an outrageous moment, Cari wished he was a chef and then she'd know he had no interest in replacing Hawthorne House with medical buildings. She lowered her gaze, watching his slender fingers reach for a shaker of hot-pepper seasoning. They were beautiful hands.

''Empty apartments make owners unhappy.'' The sound of the physician's voice tore her gaze away from his hands. She blinked. What was she thinking? They were only hands. Tools of his trade. Most surgeons had nice hands.

''Not all of the owners will be unhappy with a vacancy. If it's the lesser of two problems. Like pouring more money into paint and repairs if the house can be sold.''

''There's more than one owner?'' Dr. Carson secured the threateningly obese hamburger in his fingers.

''Two.'' Cari frowned. Funny he wouldn't know that if he was joining Dr. Barstow in buying the houses if the zoning change went through.

''Maybe I should look at the apartment, even if I can only get a short-term lease. This venture with Jim will take all the money I could beg, borrow, and save.''

Scattered thoughts fluttered in Cari's mind like tea towels in a clothes dryer. Why didn't she just come right out and ask him if he and Dr. Barstow were planning to buy Hawthorne House? Declare the battle lines—throw down the gauntlet, or whatever.

Rand's casual tone interrupted her galloping thoughts before she could vocalize them. And he changed the subject of conversation.

"Why didn't you apply for the OR when you started to work at the hospital here?"

She regained her composure in time to answer calmly. "I did, but no openings were available. I worked an evening shift on a medical floor until I was notified of a position."

"I'm glad you did. An efficient nurse makes my job easier." He motioned to the condiments. "Try some. I prefer the red sauce, but the green is pretty tasty." Rand grinned before he bit into his colorful concoction again, apparently unaware of Cari's silence.

Mechanically, Cari ladled a few drops of emerald green liquid between the layers of her sandwich, her thoughts involuntarily returning to Hawthorne House. How could she confront him with her suspicions when he was so amiable?

Anxiety overcame her reluctance. "About this venture with Dr. Barstow . . ." The words echoed in her ears as if they had traveled over raw gravel.

Chapter Three

Rand lowered his sandwich and looked at Cari.

"The medical clinic." His eyes brightened with enthusiasm. "As Jim mentioned, we planned years ago to go into practice together. The idea of the clinic came along later. Jim found what he thinks is a good location for a medical facility. He wrote me about it before I got back to Buena Vista." He nodded for a waitress to refill his glass and turned back to Cari. "A group of older houses in a downtown neighborhood. It's near the hospital, and the area's ripe for urban renewal. Ideal for what we want to do."

Cari's breath caught in her throat. Hawthorne House was only a few blocks from the hospital. It was definitely an older house. And one couldn't deny the neighborhood was due for an overhaul. Icy fragments of anxiety slid over her tense nerves.

"The houses will be torn down, of course. We're interested in the land. We want to build a state-of-the-art medical building. A facility to enhance the area as well as provide improved health care for the people."

"The people in the area have a hospital." Cari tried to keep the chill from her voice.

"Ah." Rand's smile widened. "But this will have

an outpatient surgery for minor surgeries and an evening clinic for working parents. Care in emergency rooms, which is often the only medical care available after physicians' offices close, costs a fortune, even when people have insurance. And emergency-room care isn't needed in many cases—colds, flu, minor injuries.''

He paused to take a breath. ''When a working parent comes home to find their child has a temperature, they don't wait for doctors' offices to open the next morning. Would you? Even if the cost was less?'' He didn't wait for an answer. ''We can take the load off emergency rooms and free their staff for the serious trauma cases and true emergencies.''

His zeal was so passionate that for a moment admiration tinged Cari's eyes. How could one help but admire his zeal? Didn't she tell herself the desire to help those in need was one reason she had chosen a career in nursing? Rand's plan was to make a difference in care that she could never make as a staff nurse.

With a jolt, she remembered his dream would destroy hers. ''Have you approached the owners of the property you want to buy?''

''Jim has been handling the details. But like attending the council meeting, it's time I began shouldering my share.'' Cari lifted her sandwich and took a minute bite for an excuse not to speak. He'd answered her question—even if she didn't like the answer. What did she do now? With relief, she looked up to see the waitress smiling at Rand while she ran down a memorized list of desserts for the day.

Cari shook her head at Rand's questioning look. She had to leave. She couldn't declare war with her thoughts tumbling amid an avalanche of confusion. She glanced at her watch without noting the time and mumbled something about having to get home.

''Dutch treat,'' she said quickly. She slid her share of the bill and tip across the table, quashing Rand's dissent with a humorous comment on his need to rent an apartment. She fled without a backward glance. She couldn't be beholden to the enemy for dinner.

The next morning, Cari breathed easier to find her assignment was not in Dr. Randolph Carson's room. She wanted to be mad at him, and it was difficult to work in a job she loved and be angry. Besides, each time she worked up a dram of anger, the memory of Rand's passion for his project diluted it. How could anyone condemn his professional and humanitarian goal? She slammed a lap pack on a table with more force than necessary. Why couldn't he find another location for his dream?

It was noon before she saw him. He stood by the nurses' station, scanning what looked like a report from radiology. One hand reached to remove his mask and cap to expose hair as rumpled as the scrubs stretched across his athletic body. As she approached, he looked up, his eyes brightening as if he'd been waiting for her. Before she could think of fueling an ember of anger, the beat of her heart quelled it.

''Hi.'' Rand smiled easily. ''Are you having lunch in the cafeteria?''

She grimaced humorously. ''I have another case in fifteen minutes.''

''That's enough time for a cup of coffee.''

Cari hesitated. She'd intended to have a cup of coffee, but not with the man she was trying to be mad at. ''Just about.'' She spoke hurriedly before she could change her mind.

Rand nodded toward two empty chairs at the end of the desk. ''Cream, sugar, or black?''

''Black,'' Cari said. She watched him stride to the coffeemaker, noting he'd found scrubs in a larger size today. She also noted the tunic still fitted snugly.

Rand was back in seconds, handing her a filled cup and sinking into a chair near her. ''I called the number you gave me and spoke to the manager. He agreed to let me see the apartment after office hours. I thought you might put in a good word for me.''

Cari's fingers pressed into the ceramic mug and she lowered her gaze to the coffee, daring the liquid to slosh over the rim. ''The condo is out?''

''No vacancy for thirty days. I need to move, like, yesterday.''

''Wore out your welcome?'' She was amazed she could inject a note of humor in the comment.

''Jim's wife went into labor this morning—and you know the in-laws arrived.''

''Good reasons.'' Glancing up, Cari took a sip of coffee.

''Come on.'' Rand's smile spread to his eyes. ''I hate living in hotels. Put in a good word for me.''

''You may not be so eager when you see it. I told you it needs paint and things. There's also still a chance it could be sold.''

''Sounds like a lot of buying and selling in this area.''

Cari looked away to keep from glaring at him. Did

he really not know he was trying to buy the house with the ''empty apartment''?

''Will you be in this evening?''

''I'm on second call—backup call. I doubt I'll get called for the OR this evening. So I'll be home.''

Cari stood, taking a last sip of her coffee, and walked to rinse the cup before placing it on a cart. Maybe Rand's move into Hawthorne House could be turned to her advantage. If he lived in Hawthorne House, maybe—she blocked out the thought of the former tenant who couldn't move to a nicer location fast enough—just maybe, he'd come to love it as she did. He might see the need to preserve it. Of course, it wasn't only Rand she had to thwart. Dr. Barstow, her aunt . . . but one thing at a time.

Rand lowered his coffee cup. ''About six, then?'' The devastating smile surfaced again.

Cari watched him walk toward the doctors' lounge with an odd feeling. He wanted to live across the hall and share a bathroom with her when he was threatening her dreams! He'd probably pop out his door at half past six with that devastating smile, bounce down the stairs beside her, and expound on his state-of-the-art building, looking expectantly for her enthusiastic smile.

Which he wouldn't get. However friendly, he was the foe. A point to keep in mind.

But could she afford to antagonize him openly? Disgruntled surgeons could get nurses dismissed, or at least transferred. She liked working in the operating room. But more important, she needed the extra money she could make taking call.

Clocking off duty a little after four, Cari braved the

crowded lines at the supermarket, looking forward to reaching home. She wanted to kick off her colorful shoes, plop into her one comfortable chair with a glass of iced tea, and escape into the pages of the romantic suspense novel she'd started. Her last case had been hectic.

The silver gray BMW parked in front of Ben's house stood out amid the line of less luxurious cars parked on the street. Cari maneuvered her ten-year-old Ford into a vacant spot along the curb and raised an eyebrow humorously. Ben's daughter must have gotten a substantial raise.

Ben McGrath's house, a Victorian-style structure similar to her grandmother's house, stood on a corner lot. The chipped and faded siding went unnoticed behind a riot of colorful rosebeds segregated by circular and rectangular fences of low-trimmed shrubbery. Small islands of roses extended to the backyard, separating strategically to allow a pathway to a freshly painted blue-and-white gazebo.

Arms filled with grocery bags, Cari strode around her car, across the sidewalk, and paused at the open gate in front of the house. ''Hi, Ben.''

Her gaze roved over the bushes dense with roses: white, pink, and scarlet flowers and one bush of coral blossoms the size of small cabbages preened in the late afternoon sun. Ben stood amid a circular bevy of bushes, trimming dried petals from the colorful array. ''You're looking as hale and hearty as your roses today.''

''Which may not be such a good thing.'' His pale blue eyes twinkled above a prominent nose and a gargantuan white mustache. ''I heard somewhere that a sick person can't be thrown out of their home.'' He cut a velvety red bloom and stepped outside the green-leafed barrier to present it to Cari. ''Maybe I should act like I'm ailing.''

Smiling her appreciation for the rose, Cari slipped the long-stemmed beauty carefully into one grocery bag. She closed her eyes momentarily, savoring the scent of the blossom before she answered him with a laugh. ''Pretending to be ill might be difficult the way you look today.''

''I was in a few college plays.'' He stood tall, brushed back a strand of white hair, and bent slightly in a bow.

Cari giggled. ''Don't take to your bed yet. I'm checking into the historical value of these houses.'' Her gaze strayed to the house behind the roses. To even the casual looker, it was apparent Ben spent no time on the maintenance of the sad looking house. But then, maybe the Historical Society would be so awed with the blossoms rampaging over the yard and the carefully preserved gazebo, they wouldn't notice that only a major overhaul would save the ailing structure. She looked back at Ben at the sound of a chuckle.

''Come to think of it, my acting career was short lived.'' He rolled his eyes mischievously. ''I'd consider breaking a leg, but it would interfere with my yard work.''

''Don't consider anything unusual yet. The council doesn't meet for a few weeks.'' She took another breath of the scented air. ''I've gotta run. See ya.'' She turned and strode along the walk to Hawthorne House.

In front of the house, she paused, scanning the results of her recent work. Unlike the plethora of blossoms next door, three straggly pink geranium plants sagged like neglected orphans near the freshly painted sides of the house. Cari shook her head. Next year, she'd concentrate on flowers. Roses and purple irises, yellow daffodils and big fat blossoms of pink hydrangea like the ones pictured in the nursery catalog. The geraniums could go upstairs in window boxes. She refused to consider that the house might not be hers next year.

Built in the late eighteen hundreds, the Gothic-style house needed two lots to contain its broad structure. The newly repaired steps led to a railing-enclosed porch that wrapped around one corner. High above the front door, twin gables paralleled a central gable. A smaller, fenced balcony projected beneath the scallop-trimmed central structure. Cari knew its face by heart. She cared for every aging board, although Reba teased her it had a face only a mother could love. She sighed. She should be applying a coat of paint to the scalloped trim instead of going in to read a book.

Climbing the repaired steps, she noted the stained-glass pane of red roses in the upper half of the old-fashioned door needed cleaning. The accumulated dust decorating the pane looked as though it hadn't been disturbed since she'd washed the door last month. She maneuvered a hand free and opened the door. John Branson, the elderly manager, did have a lot to do, what with caring for his wife and the plumbing and electrical problems. He'd been the manager since the house had been turned into apartments. Once Reba had suggested Cari could save money by managing the place herself, but Cari reasoned that calling a plumber at midnight might cost more than Mr. Branson's salary. Taking extra calls also meant she wasn't home often.

Inside the entry, voices traveled from the living room. Cari smiled. Maggie Branson had company. Housebound most days in a wheelchair, the middle-aged woman's delight in talking to others impelled Cari to stop to say hello each day.

Today, Cari walked purposefully past the doorway. Maggie's voice halted her in her steps.

"Cari, is that you?

"Hi, Maggie." She balanced a bag of groceries in her left arm and hesitated with one foot on a stair.

"I thought I recognized your bouncy step," the familiar voice called. "Can you come in for a minute?"

"Sure thing." Cari shifted the slipping bag and turned to walk to the parlor. At the door, she stopped.

Rand Carson lounged in one of a pair of faded velvet Victorian chairs in the crowded room. The room was furnished in much the same way Cari remembered it as a child. The Bransons had added a bit more clutter with a television set and a table and cart for Maggie's hobby supplies.

Clad in one of her colorful Hawaiian muumuus, Maggie had pushed her worktable aside, postponing the application of colorful strokes on an ebony T-shirt emblazoned with perky scarlet robins. "Cari, I think you know Dr. Carson." She smiled, waiting for Cari to acknowledge the doctor with a greeting.

"John has gone to the hardware store. Could you give the doctor a tour?" She paused expectantly.

"I'd be glad to show Dr. Carson the apartment,"

Cari said. The prospect of sinking into a chair with a tall glass of iced tea faded.

Maggie beamed. ''The door should be open. John's been cleaning in there.''

Cari nodded at the doctor. ''If you're ready, I need to put a few things in the refrigerator.'' She smiled at Maggie with added brilliance, as if she feared her dismay may have shown in her face, and dipped her head toward the work in progress on the table. ''I like the red birds.''

Rand reached for Cari's grocery bags as they approached the stairs. ''Your bluebirds are quite attractive too.'' He glanced toward the brilliantly painted T-shirt Cari wore. ''Is that some of Mrs. Branson's work?''

Cari climbed three stairs before she answered, aware of his nearness. ''This was a gift from Maggie. She was handpainting T-shirts and carryalls when I moved in. I sort of advertise to the people at the hospital.'' She turned her head to look at him briefly. ''If you're shopping for a gift, her work is on display in a local craft shop also.''

''I'll keep that in mind.'' Rand's voice came over her right shoulder.

At the top of the stairs, she stepped onto the landing and nodded at the first door on the left. ''Let me drop off the groceries.'' She pulled a key from her purse and slid it into the new lock above the tarnished doorknob. ''The apartments aren't as modern as the locks.'' She turned the key and twisted the knob. The door didn't move. ''Gran had a long, thin key that resembled a miniature pole with a metal flag on one end. Not that I remember her using it often. She once said she forgot to lock the door when they went on a month's vacation and nothing was disturbed when they returned.'' She laughed nervously. ''Though I don't imagine one could leave one's door unlocked a month these days. Or a day, for that matter.''

Relieved when the door opened at the next push, Cari curtailed her vocal rambling and stepped aside to allow Rand to enter. ''You can drop that bag of groceries on the table.'' She followed him through the door and went past him to place her bag on the kitchen counter.

Rand shifted the bulging bag and turned to survey the living room and mini-kitchen. ''Nice.''

''The apartment across the hall is similar to this.''

Sweeping one hand toward the mini-kitchen, she grinned. ''Kitchen.'' She moved her arm to encompass the rest of the room. ''Living room. The other room is the bedroom. I warned you it was no swinging-singles abode. No swimming pool, no spa, no weight room. What you see is what you get.''

''You didn't mention the dining room.'' He nodded at the small round table covered with a pink floor-length cloth overlaid with a crocheted circle of lace.

''Cardboard assemble-it-yourself furniture, a bed-sheet cut to fit, and a doily from the thrift shop. The two chairs are from my grandmother's dining set.''

Rand walked across the room to peer over the waist-high partition at the kitchen area. ''Microwave oven, toaster, even a sink. What more could a person want?''

''Hot water.''

''You don't have water?'' The sparkle in his eyes barely wavered. ''I can get used to that.''

''We have water. It's not hot.''

"Is this it?

A faint flush heated Cari's face. "The bedroom." Cari pointed to a closed door without looking at Rand. "There were four bedrooms on the second floor, and Gran had them remodeled into apartments while she still lived here. She left two bedrooms intact—even the furniture is the same. But the other two bedrooms became a living room–kitchen arrangement."

Cari stepped back as Rand stepped in the kitchen area and lowered the grocery bag to the counter. Cari felt the microwave pressing into her back. The kitchenette seemed to be decreasing in space and increasing in temperature. She retrieved two frozen packages from the bag and opened the freezer compartment of her small refrigerator. Chilled air flowing from the icy interior touched her heated skin. She lowered her parcels to the ledge and rearranged the packages inside needlessly. It wasn't the unexpected appearance of the handsome doctor, or his proximity, that unnerved her, she told herself. Hadn't she always tried to grab a few minutes to unwind between the hospital and the next task? This was one of those days when she hadn't succeeded. It had happened before. So why wasn't she coping better today?

Unable to hide behind the door longer, Cari put the milk and juice cartons away quickly and turned to Rand. "Thank you for waiting." Instead of squeaking, her voice came out with the impersonal tone of a preprogrammed telephone message. "I'm sure you're anxious to see the other apartment?" She smiled, her look bouncing off Rand's face.

Crossing the hall, Cari opened the unlocked door and preceded Rand inside. She walked to the middle of the room before stopping. ''Not much furniture.'' She made a wry face at a faded sofa. ''Kaye left the sofa because it wouldn't go with her new apartment. The mini-fridge goes with the place.'' She watched him walk around the room with mixed feelings as he cheerfully examined the refrigerator and turned on the tap above the small sink.

How could they be neighbors when he was destined to be her enemy? Neighbors were supposed to be friendly.

''Hey,'' he interrupted her thoughts. ''With a toaster and a coffeepot, I'll feel like I live in a mansion.''

Involuntarily, a smile softened Cari's face. How could anyone not find some tolerance for a man so cheerful and amiable? Even an admission of a little attraction. One more exhibit of his unique smile that encompassed his whole face and her determination to stay clear of any serious romantic involvement could be in jeopardy.

The thought startled her. Even if she could overcome her antipathy to marriage, Rand was the enemy. She glanced away and noted a new chair in the room.

''Looks like John found you a chair.'' Cari nodded at the straight-backed chair near the wall. If he can find another one not in use downstairs, you could have company.''

''I could even serve cold drinks''—Rand looked at the refrigerator—''if the fridge works.''

''It should. But this is no party pad.''

''It's fine. I won't be here that long.''

Cari widened her eyes questioningly, but deep inside, she anticipated his answer.

''This is part of the property Jim and I plan to buy.

It'll be torn down in less than six months if everything goes well.''

Pain seared through Cari. How could he say it so casually? She cleared her throat. ''I thought you wanted to wait until the zoning was changed before you seriously considered buying the properties on this block.''

Rand opened the door to the bedroom and looked in.

''The realtor thinks we can overcome the roadblocks. He sent offers to all the owners. Only a couple of them are being obstinate.''

Cari pursed her lips. Obstinate. How about immovable? ''I know. I received a letter.''

''Oh?'' Rand looked at her in surprise.

''My grandmother left this house to my aunt and me,'' she said stiffly.

Rand grinned. ''Maybe we can lure your aunt with money.''

''It's not my aunt...'' The sound of the beeper clipped to Rand's belt interrupted her.

Rand reached to his waist to silence the sound and looked at Cari. ''May I use your telephone?''

He crossed the room and followed Cari across the hall. She waited in the doorway, glaring at his back as he picked up the phone. Money *was* a lure, she thought, recalling his words. But to repair Hawthorne House, not sell it for demolition.

When he turned after making the brief call, she wondered if she should walk downstairs with him. She'd done her duty. Shown him the apartment. Was she expected to do more? But he stood waiting for her to move, and she preceded him down the stairs and into the Bransons' living room. Maggie had halted the work on the T-shirt in front of her to look at the nineteen-inch television screen displaying a Rockford rerun.

Cari glanced at the surgeon. She had to correct his impression about her aunt, to tell him she was the obstinate owner and she could be as dedicated to her cause as the proverbial mailman. Neither rain nor sleet nor snow could deter her from her course. She grinned wryly. In California, it was more likely to be fire, flood, or earthquake, but she didn't plan to let them stop her either. Maggie looked up and smiled at the doctor before Cari could speak.

"It's a lovely apartment," Maggie said, as if Dr. Carson might be hesitant. "Did you look at the view of the mountains from the balcony?"

Cari smiled weakly. Maggie, too, was unwilling to admit to the possibility that the place would be demolished.

"Very nice," Rand said. "When will it be available for me to move in?"

"This weekend, I would think. You like it, then?" she added, as if to confirm his words.

"It has everything. A bed, a chair, a refrigerator—and a friendly neighbor." His grinned endearingly at the prospective neighbor stalling the still half-prepared speech tumbling in her thoughts.

Cari's heart felt like it was doing broad jumps in a high school athletic meet. Telling herself he was the enemy didn't keep her from being strongly attracted to Rand Carson. Nor grudgingly admiring his plans for the clinic.

Chapter Four

Cari entered the nurses' lounge at a quarter to four, halting in surprise at the sight of half a dozen OR people in the room. On Fridays, most employees rushed for the exits as though a 50-percent-off sale was being held in the parking lot.

Smiling a general greeting, she poured herself a cup of coffee and looked for a place to rest.

"What day shall I put your name on the calendar, Cari?"

Cari refocused her gaze and blinked at the surgical technician poising a pencil over a sheet of notepaper.

"Are you doing the call schedule this week?"

"What?" The technician looked up as if she'd been daydreaming. "Oh, the on-call schedule? No. I'm asking which evening you want to make a casserole for Dr. Carson."

Cari frowned and Reba laughed.

"Apparently you haven't heard about the food rescue squad," Reba said lightly.

"No, I haven't heard about the food rescue squad, but I gather I'm about to become a member, so enlighten me."

Reba grinned mischievously. "It seems Dr. Carson

regaled the surgery crew on the late shift with the adventures of a bachelor in a new residence. Dr. Barstow's wife has supplied him with bedding, so he isn't sleeping on the floor. But the poor dear is living on peanut butter sandwiches and instant coffee made with tepid tap water.'' Reba shook her head sadly, but the corners of her mouth twitched. ''He hasn't had time to shop for a coffeepot.''

''Living on peanut butter?'' Cari's laughter rippled across the room. ''He didn't move in until Thursday evening.''

''So maybe he said he might have to live on peanut butter and lukewarm coffee,'' the technician said grumpily. ''Would it hurt us to welcome him to Buena Vista with a little neighborly casserole or two?''

Cari lowered her gaze, concentrating on the dark liquid in her cup. She could have offered Rand the use of her microwave when she'd heard Maggie explain that her husband had sent the old one out for repairs. But having Rand Carson live next door was bad enough. The thought of him running in and out of her kitchen was downright unnerving. Besides, Maggie had offered the doctor the use of the downstairs kitchen until the oven was returned.

Another nurse leaned forward, smiling at Cari. ''Some of the gals in the OR thought it would be nice to take Dr. Carson a casserole for a few days—maybe a week—until he can buy something to cook in, not to mention cook on.''

Feeling the gaze of the others in the lounge looking at her expectantly, Cari buoyed her spirits with a sip of coffee before she spoke. ''I'm on call from now until seven tomorrow morning. What's available after that?''

''This evening is taken care of and we're not doing the weekend. Dr. Carson is taking call. Besides, someone heard Dr. Barstow ask him to dinner Sunday.''

''Check the schedule and put me down for any day I'm not on call,'' Cari said with more confidence than she felt. She vaguely remembered making a tuna casserole once with her mother. It stood out because her mother hadn't been big on cooking either. She took another sip of coffee and tried to recall seeing something that could be called a casserole in the frozen-food section of the supermarket.

As the others stood, Cari refilled her cup and looked at Reba. ''Have coffee with me. I'm in no rush to leave. I haven't checked with the ER or the surgical floor yet to see if there might be a case pending.''

''Sure.'' Reba leaned back against the well-used couch.

Nodding to departing personnel, Cari handed Reba a cup of coffee, took a swallow from her own cup, and returned to her chair. ''I'm waiting to hear about the date with the physical therapist.'' Humor sparkled in her eyes.

Reba sighed dreamily. ''I'm ready to take him home to meet my dad.''

''But is he ready to go?'' Cari teased.

''I plan to work on that—slowly. He's an only child.''

''Cari chuckled. ''So don't take him home to dinner until you warn him the dining table at your house is a fold-down conference-room table for twenty.''

Reba chuckled. ''We seldom have twenty people for

dinner. It only seems that way when seven children—and a playmate or two—sit down.''

''Your parents are exceptional.'' A wave of emotion swept through Cari. Reba's parent's had given the four children of her father's brother a home after their parents had died in an accident.

''I think so.'' Reba grinned. ''Especially Mom. I feel guilty sometimes about moving into town to be nearer the hospital. But Mom says my teenage brother and sister and my niece help with the younger children.''

''Shades of *The Brady Bunch* and *Little House*, huh?'' Cari said. She didn't allow a tinge of wistfulness in her voice. ''Think the PT hunk likes children?''

Reba wrinkled her nose humorously. ''Can't tell. From what I learned about his parents, they are confirmed professionals who believe children should be seen seldom and heard less. Which means Greg's pretty quiet. I don't know how he'll feel about my boisterous family.'' She grinned broadly. ''But I'll find out next Sunday.''

''You're taking Greg to dinner?''

''Might as well see how the wind blows before I really fall for him.'' She sighed dreamily. ''Enough of my daily drama. How was your council meeting?''

''The zoning issue was postponed until the council meets again.'' Cari elaborated on the tardy attorney.

''But that's only a postponement. What are you doing that's positive?''

Cari sipped coffee for a minute before she spoke. ''A Historical Society member spoke on another issue, but it did give me an idea about stressing the importance of Hawthorne House's historical value. Maybe I can look into that aspect. Meanwhile . . .'' Cari scowled. ''You'll never guess the identities of the villains planning to demolish Hawthorne House.''

''Some business conglomerate planning to build offices, you said.''

Cari sighed heavily. ''Drs. Barstow and Carson. They plan to build a clinic and an outpatient surgery center.''

Reba scowled. ''Neither of them is a likely villain. Are you sure?''

''Straight from the doctor's mouth.''

''Did you tell him you're opposed to selling?''

''Nooo.'' Cari strung the word out. ''Somehow, the right time to tell him I owned half of Hawthorne House kept moving forward.''

''Tell him,'' Reba said succinctly. ''Better yet, tell him how you feel about it.''

''Little good that would do. Not to mention making it harder to work with him.''

Reba pursed her lips wryly. ''It doesn't make it any easier having him move into the apartment across from you, does it?''

''I did have a little idea about that.'' Cari pressed the small gold earring in her left ear to ascertain she hadn't pulled it off with her paper cap. ''He said he liked friendly neighbors, and you know the residents of Hawthorne House. The Bransons started the barbecue dinner we have every Saturday evening. John built a ramp off the rear porch so his wife can push her wheelchair to the backyard. Ben from next door joins us most times. Plus the Greens on the next block who take Ben with them to church, and you when you're on call and not going home for the weekend. Then Maggie loves to have people in the parlor for coffee on Sunday afternoons. If Dr. Carson becomes involved with the people in the house . . .'' She lifted her shoulders. ''It's not even a plan yet. But if he could see the house like I do, he wouldn't want to destroy it. Would he?''

Reba looked at her friend compassionately. ''I think that's a line to explore further. Meanwhile, contact this Historical Society. And petitions. Did you think about petitions? I've signed petitions for saving land for animals, wildlife, and nature lovers. Why not for home owners?'' She stood up slowly. ''Hate to leave you, but I'm going home this weekend and I promised Mom I'd do some shopping for her before I came.''

Cari nodded in understanding. She rose, reached for Reba's cup, and took it to the bathroom sink to rinse. ''Have a good weekend.''

Reba opened the door and waved a raised hand. ''You too.''

Cari used paper towels to wipe the cups before replacing them on a plastic tray. A fleeting feeling of loneliness assailed her. It must be nice to have a family to visit on weekends. She hadn't seen her mother for over a year; she hadn't even talked to her for four months. The last time her mother had called, she'd been on her way to the Bahamas. The band her husband was with had a three-week engagement to play at a nightclub. She sighed. Maybe her newest stepfather would get a gig in California one of these days. She opened the door of the lounge and headed for the emergency room.

*   *   *

Rand handed the check to the rental car clerk and waited for the attractive dark-haired woman to locate the keys to a Honda Accord. It was his first day off since he'd arrived in Buena Vista. So why wasn't he jumping for joy instead of feeling so restless?

He'd arisen twenty minutes later than usual. By the time he'd showered and dressed, he'd missed Cari. Not that he had anything earth shattering to say to her. But her perky smile and cheerful voice started his day off well. He'd strolled out to the curved balcony, carrying his tepid cup of instant coffee, and caught a glimpse of her middle-aged car as she pulled away from the curb. She hadn't looked back, so he'd lowered the hand that had been ready to wave.

He made patient rounds at the hospital. He stopped in the doctors' lounge and chatted with an older physician, the only man in the room. He shopped for a coffeepot and an oven toaster. Dropping his purchases in the car, he slid behind the steering wheel. A minute later, he routed the car toward Hawthorne House.

The route also went within a block of the hospital. He glanced at his wristwatch, a tentative surge of hunger teasing him. It was near noon, and his breakfast had been two cups of coffee. He ignored the taste buds craving for French fries and a colossal bacon burger. The food in the hospital dining room was healthier. Whether or not Cari Masterson took her usual lunch break in the dining room was incidental.

Two surgical techs ate between bouts of animated conversation, but Rand's searching gaze found no nurses from the operating room. With an inexplicable feeling of apathy, he left the hospital to go to the office and look at the appointment book for the following day. He stopped in to chat with Jim. All the while, the hands on his wristwatch seemed to move so slowly, he wondered if his watch needed a new battery.

He took a detour on the way to his new home. The Yuba River was less than two miles from the hospital, though it couldn't be seen from any of the offices or patient rooms. He wished it could. He missed the river. Checking the traffic behind him, Rand signaled and made a turn off the road onto a parkway overlooking the water.

He'd thought of the flowing water more than once when he'd been far from his boyhood home. The water rippling past him now flowed past the ranch his parents owned farther north. He took a deep breath. Or what there was left of his parents' property. His dad had insisted on selling a large part of the acreage to enable him to lend Rand money for the clinic project. Rand gazed reflectively at the flowing water. His dad's trust in the project was just one of the reasons it had to succeed.

The small hand on Rand's watch pointed near four when he carried his purchases up the front steps of the Victorian house. On the porch, Mrs. Branson sat in her wheelchair reading.

''I see you like biographies.'' He nodded at the hardback book in her hand. He leaned closer and scanned the title. ''I haven't found time to read much lately, but biographies are one of my favorites.''

Smiling, Maggie relocated a bookmark and closed the book. ''My husband goes to the local library once a week and has the librarian choose books for me.''

Rand nodded, resting his purchases on the railing. "I've been shopping."

Maggie looked at the image of the toaster oven on the large box. "We're sorry about the microwave. I know it's inconvenient to come downstairs to use the oven."

"Don't worry about it. With a coffeepot and a toaster oven, I might manage a two-course dinner."

Maggie smiled at him warmly. "Which you won't have to do this evening. Two nurses from the operating room delivered a casserole a few minutes ago. I had them put it in the fridge in the kitchen." She placed the book on a nearby rattan table. "They seemed disappointed that you weren't here."

Rand repositioned the cardboard cartons, taking a moment to assess the older lady. Teasing him had brought a sparkle to Mrs. Branson's eyes. "Does that mean you think I should invite the ladies from the casserole care committee to share my dinner?" His voice was equally teasing.

Maggie's smile was totally unembarrassed. "Being selective wouldn't hurt."

Rand grinned. No way would he ask what selection she thought he should make. Still grinning, he picked up his purchases and strode toward the door. "I'll come back for the dish after I take these things upstairs. Be right back," he said over his shoulder.

Depositing the boxes, he went to the bedroom, removing his jacket as he walked. He hung the light jacket in the closet, looked at the unmade bed, and decided it could wait another hour. Who would see it? He chuckled to himself. Certainly not Cari Masterson. She was not the casual-affair type. Or maybe any kind of ''affair'' type. He wondered if she gave every man mixed signals, or was it just him?

He returned to his kitchenette, opening the refrigerator to find room for another casserole. He grimaced. Monday and Tuesday's leftovers filled the small space. Putting them together might leave space for another dish. Closing both the refrigerator door and the apartment door, he went downstairs.

Maggie's voice came from a distance as he entered the living room. ''I'm in the kitchen,'' she called.

Sidestepping the older lady's hobby table, Rand strode through the dining room to the large kitchen. A tremor of warmth washed over him when he opened the swinging doors. At the counter, Cari stood spooning coffee into a coffee maker.

Maggie Branson looked up from her position by the round oak table in the center of the room. ''Cari and I are going to sample a new coffee flavor. Will you join us?''

''Hazel Nut Crème today.'' Cari turned, meeting Rand's gaze briefly but sending a smile that increased the spread of warmth.

''Hazel Nut Crème sounds too tempting to turn down. What can I do to help?'' He crossed the room to halt beside her, aware of the curves barely concealed by today's gaily decorated T-shirt.

She busied her hands with the coffee maker. ''Uh, cups.'' Her voice wavered. ''You'll find them in the cupboard on my right. Sugar''—her voice became stronger—''is in the next cupboard over. Cream in the fridge.''

''Spoons in the drawer near Cari.'' Mrs. Branson's

vocal addition surprised him. He'd almost forgotten she was in the room.

"Right." Rand recovered quickly. He glanced at the spoon drawer, half-hidden by Cari's shorts-clad hip, and moved to the refrigerator. A little space while searching for the cream pitcher might cool his hormones.

Seconds later, he closed the refrigerator door and his gaze involuntarily swung to Cari. She'd turned to talk to Mrs. Branson, and her melodic voice pulled at his heartstrings. Lowering his eyes before she could look his way, he let his gaze wander downward and encountered an assortment of shimmery seashells scattered across a curvy patch of violet cloth, a pair of navy walking shorts, and violet-hued, shell-spattered tennies. He let out a breath. Her decorative attire and animated voice were far different from the cool, efficient role she assumed in the operating room.

He pulled his thoughts back to the kitchen and moved to the cabinet to search for cups and saucers. Only when he placed a rose-decorated sugar bowl on the table did he notice he hadn't matched one dish. He raised a glance heavenward. Good thing T-shirts and shorts weren't standard operating room attire for Cari!

"Spoons." Ignoring an impish internal voice, he gave Cari ample warning before he invaded her space.

Cari started, stepping aside to let the aroma of brewing coffee filter between them. He watched her open the drawer, withdraw four spoons, and raise blue eyes, still sparkling from the laughter over Maggie's last quip, to his. It doubled the intensity as his fingers closed over the spoons and touched hers. For a moment, neither hand moved.

''The round one is for the sugar bowl.'' Cari released the silverware abruptly.

Fingers still tingling from her touch, Rand turned his attention to Mrs. Branson. ''I forgot to thank you for the loan of the dishes yesterday.''

She looked up from rearranging a low bowl of flowers that resembled the roses growing in the yard next door. ''Plastic forks and paper plates don't add much to the flavor of food, do they?''

Rand chuckled. ''They aren't too sturdy either.'' He moved around the table, aware of Cari crossing the room with the coffee carafe. She reached for a mismatched cup, filled it, and passed it to Mrs. Branson before she looked at him. ''How was yesterday's casserole?'' she asked, the words tinged with humor.

Rand closed his eyes briefly and made a pleased sound. ''Whoever sent it is going to make someone a great wife.'' He didn't try to conceal his look of admiration. He liked the way Cari Masterson looked out of uniform. He liked her smile, he liked her sense of humor, and he liked her efficiency in the operating room. If she was the one who'd sent yesterday's casserole, he might have to reconsider his reluctance to enter a relationship before he'd established a medical practice. ''But how do I know whom to thank? The hospital personnel leave the dishes with Mrs. Branson with a message to return the dishes to the surgery department.''

Cari's smile and the sound of her throaty laughter teased him. ''If there isn't a Post-it note on top, check the bottom of the dish when you wash it. The person who sends it usually puts a name somewhere so she can reclaim the dish.''

''Aah.'' Rand nodded in understanding.

''She or he,'' Cari amended. ''That delicious carrot cake that shows up for the OR crew occasionally is made by Matt Field.''

Rand slid a cup toward her. Carrot cake wasn't his favorite dessert, but with Cari smiling at him as though the concoction was the pot of gold at the end of the rainbow, he'd swallow every crumb.

''So, are you going to make me climb the stairs and look at the bottom of the dish to see who made that casserole? Or do I just return the dish to my nearest neighbor?''

''Me!'' Cari's laughter rippled across the rose bouquet. ''I'm good at opening a can of tuna, but I get lost after that.'' She paused for effect. ''Reba made it.''

Any disappointment that Cari hadn't made the dish fled. So what if she couldn't cook. ''Reba is the nurse whose family has a big farm outside of town.''

''That's her. Big farm, big family, big heart.''

Big heart. Somehow, the title fitted Cari. Mrs. Branson had mentioned Cari's frequent visits and her concern about the elderly neighbor who grew roses. He watched her pull another mismatched cup toward her.

''Reba says she grew up helping her mother turn yesterday's dinner into a casserole supreme, so I knew it had to be good.''

''It was delicious.'' Rand stirred sugar into the steaming liquid in his cup, searching for a topic to keep Cari talking. ''My folks own a big farm too, farther north. That is, they did own a big farm.'' He shook his head at Mrs. Branson's offer of the cream pitcher.

''Did own a big farm?'' Mrs. Branson echoed.

He slid the sugar bowl toward Cari and sat down as she did. ''Dad had four hundred acres. He sold most of the land.'' He took a sip of coffee and grinned broadly in appreciation. ''Great flavor.'' He set the cup down. ''I don't know if he minded too much. Farming is hard work and not necessarily a money-making proposition. If it isn't too dry, it's too wet. If it isn't the threat of brush fires, it's the inability to hire enough workers to get in the crop before the rains come. Or the price of hay falls and you plant beets and the beet market plummets.''

Maggie sighed. ''John says if it isn't the roof that needs fixing, it's the plumbing or the electricity.'' She spooned sugar into her coffee. ''I guess it all boils down to what you like to do. If growing things is your passion, you put up with the problems.''

Rand smiled wryly. ''I don't know that Dad liked to farm. He was in his second year of medical school when his father had a stroke. He went home to help with the crop that year and never returned. He didn't make a big deal of not finishing medical school, but somehow, his dream influenced me.''

''That's admirable,'' Cari said.

Rand raised one hand and fidgeted with an itch on an earlobe. ''Well, it makes the success of the clinic project even more important.''

The sound of a beeper rose above the conversation, and both Rand and Cari looked at the miniature black boxes they carried. He looked at her compassionately as she stood up.

Cari stood up with a faint feeling of relief. One more second and she'd have said something to Rand about his precious project that wasn't ladylike. Let alone conducive to continued employment in the operating room.

Maggie touched Cari's hand. "I left the telephone in the living room on my hobby table."

Cari nodded, knowing she referred to the mobile phone she usually kept near her.

When Cari returned to the kitchen, Maggie looked up inquiringly. "One of those ASAP calls, or do you have time for a fresh cup of coffee?"

Cari looked at her near empty cup. "The evening supervisor. One of the surgeons has scheduled a case for seven o'clock."

"So you have time for more coffee." Rand was striding to retrieve the coffee carafe before Cari could respond. He filled her cup, turned to replace the carafe, and his beeper sounded.

"I thought Dr. Barstow was on call this evening." Cari raised an eyebrow.

"Jim's wife was having contractions when I saw him this afternoon. I told him I'd be around if he needed me." He paused in the doorway. "Could be Jim telling me he's taking his wife to the hospital."

"Let's hope she isn't having false labor pains like last time," Cari called after Rand who was already striding toward the living room.

When he returned, he drained his cup before smiling at his hostess. "Dr. Barstow asked the nurses to call me to look at a fractured ankle." He turned to Cari with a woeful look. "And I was going to ask you to help me eat this evening's casserole."

''Your refrigerator must be overflowing.'' Cari grinned.

''I don't know where I'm going to put one more dish.'' He matched her grin. ''I meant to store two together or something.'' He looked at his watch.

Cari chuckled. ''Go on to the ER. I'll take your casserole up and find a place for it.''

''The door's unlocked,'' Rand said.

''Nice young man,'' Maggie said after Rand had left. She grinned. ''I think he has more than a professional feeling for you.''

''Umm,'' Cari demurred. Rand was attractive in more ways than one, but the problem of the house loomed between them. ''More likely, he thinks if he gets friendly, he can persuade me to sell Hawthorne House.''

Mrs. Branson sipped her coffee slowly. Replacing the cup on the table, she looked at Cari compassionately. ''I wish he could find another location too.'' She shook her head. ''He told me his dad sold part of his ranch to lend him the money so he and Dr. Barstow can buy the land for their clinic.'' She sighed. ''He is so enthusiastic and so dedicated, I find it hard to be mad at him, even if it means we'll have to move.''

Cari stared silently at her cup, her thoughts as gloomy as the dark liquid inside it.

''I know it's different for you, dear. This house means so much to you.''

Cari's lips curved in a grim smile. It wouldn't take much for Maggie to slip over to the opposition. She rose and carried her cup to the sink, returned for Rand's cup, and looked at Maggie inquiringly.

"I'll just finish my coffee while I wait for John to come in and help with dinner."

Cari nodded and returned to the sink to wash the soiled cups and place them in the dish drainer.

"If we do have to move," Maggie said humorously, "I hope we have a dishwasher in the next place."

The grin Cari gave Mrs. Branson was automatic. She couldn't take her ill disposition out on her friend—even if dishwashers weren't on her wish list today. Walking to the refrigerator, she withdrew a colorful, covered casserole dish and balanced it in both hands. "I'll put this in Rand's fridge." She pushed the refrigerator door closed with her elbow. "Thanks for the coffee. I like that flavor."

"Let's try that Swiss chocolate you bought me tomorrow." Maggie hesitated. "Or whenever you have time."

Cari nodded. She made time for Maggie more often than she should. But then, what was a few minutes taken from painting the old house? The peeling boards would be there tomorrow. Gloom surfaced momentarily again. Or would they? She stomped up the stairs, thinking dark thoughts of Dr. Randolph Carson.

Her dark thoughts didn't keep her from collecting plastic containers from her kitchen and transferring the leftover casserole into them. She slid the newer dish into the empty space in the refrigerator and glanced at her watch. She had time for a shower. That might cool her skin, but could it settle the unrest that had started with Rand's look and increased when he came near her? She closed the door to his apartment. She had to keep her mind on her problem, not his proximity.

Chapter Five

Cari entered the hospital through the emergency room door, wondering if Dr. Carson's patient with the injured ankle might be a surgery case. She halted at the sight of a familiar face. Ben McGrath sat in one of the plastic-covered chairs in the crowded waiting room.

She caught her breath, anxiety flitting through her. She scanned his face and body quickly. No sign of blood. No sign of bones protruding through a shirt-sleeve. She released her breath.

''Ben.'' She let a teasing tone cover her concern. ''This is a bad time to put on your 'ailing' act. The emergency room gets so busy after six that the personnel can't appreciate your efforts.''

The elderly man grinned. ''Glad you warned me. I'll keep it in mind to consult you about 'curtain time' for my big moment.''

''So, what's your problem today?'' Cari said pleasantly.

Ben's grin slipped. ''Guess I've been working with the roses longer than usual. My arms are a little achy and I didn't sleep well last night.'' He looked away as if embarrassed at admitting a frailty.

Cari reassessed his face. He did look tired. ''There is a little flu going around.'' She reached to touch his forehead. ''You don't seem overly warm.''

''Just achy, as I said. My arms.'' He shrugged his left shoulder.

Cari grimaced inwardly. At Ben's age, pain in his arms could mean more than overwork in his garden— or the flu. She looked up as a nurse approached.

''Hi, Barbara. Anyone in the ER who might go to surgery?''

The nurse shook her head.

''Good. I have a case scheduled. Hope that's it for the night.'' Cari placed her hand on Ben's shoulder. ''This is my friend, Mr. McGrath. He tells me he's been overdoing it in his rose garden and can't sleep at night. Take good care of him.'' She turned back to Ben. ''I have to go to work. I'll stop in and see you after I get off. That is if the lights are still on in your house.'' She paused. ''Do you want me to call your daughter?''

''And let her scold me for working too long in the yard?'' He rolled his eyes weakly. ''I'll be fine soon as I get a sleeping pill or something.''

Concern still nagged at Cari. True, Ben might have the flu, but . . . She tamped down her anxiety. The doctor on duty this evening was competent enough to differentiate between flu symptoms and something more serious.

She touched Ben's arm. ''Don't hesitate to call me tonight if you need me.'' She gave him a mock severe look and strode through the emergency room. ''You know I mean it.''

Moving toward the exit door, she saw Rand beside

a gurney where an attractive woman rested with her leg in a cast. A young man hovered over the woman, and Rand's attention was focused on the distraught couple. Cari felt a slight twinge of disappointment that he didn't notice her.

She found the surgical tech opening a sterile pack when she walked into the room. "Hi, Matt," she greeted the male tech. "The emergency room is overflowing, but Barbara said no one looks like a surgical candidate and this appendectomy shouldn't take long. We may get out of here early tonight."

"I wouldn't complain if we didn't," Matt replied. "The wife's car is in the shop with a crack in the radiator, and the dentist said our oldest girl needs braces on her teeth. We could use the extra money."

Cari chuckled. "I know what you mean." She helped set up the room and left to get the patient before the anesthetist arrived.

The surgery went smoothly, but Cari had barely transferred the patient to the recovery room before the evening supervisor called about an emergency C-section.

Cari's fingers tightened on the telephone. "Do you have a patient name?" She forced her fingers to relax. Just because Dr. Barstow's wife had been having contractions didn't mean she was the patient.

"Hold on, I'll check."

Seconds later, the supervisor said, "Hawkins." Cari relaxed, making notes as the voice added additional information.

After transferring the patient to recovery following an uneventful surgery, Cari returned to help Matt.

"I hope you made enough to get your wife's car

out of hock, because even the lure of a fatter paycheck couldn't make me enthusiastic about another case right now.''

''I'm a little bushed too,'' Matt admitted humorously.

''Then let's get out of here.'' Cari tossed disposables into a bin. A cup of hot tea seemed terribly enticing.

It was near midnight when Cari left the hospital. With a brief thought of the casserole in Rand's fridge, she went through the Taco Hut drive-thru.

She wasn't surprised to see the lights out at Ben's house. He should have been home hours ago and sleeping soundly by now. She'd forgotten to stop in the ER and ask the nurse about his diagnosis. Even flu could be serious in elderly people.

Climbing the stairs hurriedly, she stopped suddenly at the upper landing. Rand strolled down the hall clad in a mammoth towel wrapped sarong-style around his hips. The cloth extended to his ankles, leaving his bare chest with its mat of dark hair exposed.

He, too, halted his stride, his eyes radiating pleasure. ''You've had a long day.'' His voice was husky.

Cari raised her gaze quickly from his bare chest to the hair on his head. Darkened by dampness, and glistening in the overhead light, the curling tendrils did little to quell the drumbeat echoing in her own chest. She pursed her lips. Why did he have to look at her with such a devastating smile, as if he was delighted to see her, when she was too tired to rally her defenses?

''Looks like you may have also just come in.'' Cari struggled to keep her gaze above his bare chest.

''I stayed with Jim in the maternity waiting room.'' He grinned broadly. ''Seven-pound boy. Mother, father, and grandparents doing well.''

Pleasure flowed through Cari. ''That's great.''

Rand nodded at the food bag in Cari's hand. ''Today's casserole is warming in the toaster oven. How about bringing your food in and joining me?''

Cari hesitated, arching her tired shoulders.

''I picked up a package of salad mix and a bottle of dressing at the supermarket.''

Cari's weariness produced a giggle. ''How can I turn down a salad you tossed with your own hands?''

''Good.'' He opened the door and waited for her to enter.

The drumbeat in her chest picked up speed, and Cari halted inside. She gestured toward a card table and two folding chairs. ''Such splendor. My first dining room set was two apple crates and a cardboard carton that had encased the Bransons' TV set.''

He grinned. ''The table is on loan from Jim and the chairs are courtesy of the Bransons.''

Cari placed her food bag on the table with the ridiculous feeling she was floating on air. She should be kicking off her shoes and heading for bed when she was too tired to bolster her resistance to Rand's charm.

Rand interrupted her effort to think rationally. ''Just let me slip into something less comfortable.''

His grin eroded her resistance further. Watching him leave the room, Cari knew she should be in her own apartment. Maybe even taking another shower.

Rand insisted Cari sample the casserole, and she insisted he share her tacos. The salad dressing was blue cheese, the least of Cari's favorites, but it tasted delicious.

"I'm glad your 'ankle' patient didn't require surgery. We had a C-section after the appy."

"Me too. Especially when Jim came by to say he'd brought his wife in earlier." He chuckled. "Despite being a doctor and the father of a three-year-old, I do believe he was more nervous than a first-time father."

"It was nice of you to stay."

He shrugged his shoulders lightly. "It wasn't all compassion. The aroma of a fresh pot of coffee provided by a volunteer was irresistible." He pulled back the paper exposing a crisp taco shell and took a bite. "Mm. I like your caterer. You're going to have to give me his name." He exposed more tortilla.

"I'm beginning to think you like anything that's eatable." Which was good. Just in case she ever invited him to dinner. Cari felt the smile on her lips crinkling her eyes.

"Have you heard that good company improves the taste of the food?" His eyes sparkled teasingly.

"I must admit this casserole is worthy of mention."

Rand rolled his eyes. "When do nurses find the time to learn to cook? Especially OR nurses. I see them back on duty at all hours when they take call."

"Maybe that's why the ones with families make casseroles so well. They can cook a few on their day off and freeze them for emergencies."

"And what do you do?"

"I drop by my favorite drive-thru and have the chef whip up the special for the day. On rare occasions, I even eat in the dining room when I'm on call."

"Speaking of the hospital, as I was leaving, I saw

our neighbor in the emergency room. The elderly man with the rose garden . . .''

Cari's forehead wrinkled in perplexity. ''He was still at the hospital?''

Rand nodded. ''Isn't he the one who spoke against the zoning change at the council meeting?''

''Yes.'' Cari felt a spark of irritation.

''One of my opponents,'' Rand said lightly. ''Still, he didn't look too hostile tonight.''

Cari frowned. ''Ben doesn't have a hostile bone in his body, but he does cherish his wife's rose garden. And if you think a little flu, or even pneumonia, is going to make him surrender and sell his house, you're mistaken.''

''Maybe he won't have a choice,'' Rand said soberly.

Cari's irritation caught fire. ''He isn't the only one opposed to the sale of his house. Hawthorne House isn't for sale either.''

''I know. Your aunt.''

''Not my aunt. Me.'' Cari was more surprised at the boldness in her voice than the chilly tone. ''I'm the one who doesn't want to sell.'' Ignoring the look of astonishment on his face, she stood up and shoved the discarded taco wrappers into the empty paper bag. ''Thanks for sharing the casserole.'' She could barely say the words in a civil tone. ''Ben should be home by now.'' She turned and strode toward the door.

''I don't think so,'' Rand said quietly.

Cari stopped and turned around. Her anger waned in a rush of anxiety. ''He was in the waiting room when I went in for the first surgery. That was hours ago.''

"Someone should have seen him then," Rand said bluntly.

A chill swept through Cari's chest. "He said he felt achy . . . the flu."

"Pale, perspiring, clutching his left arm." Rand looked at Cari solemnly. "The nurse was transferring him to the cardiac room."

With a feeling of panic, Cari hurried out of Rand's room and down the stairs. She didn't realize she had the bag of empty taco wrappers until she flung the bag in the car.

Cari was going so fast, she had to halt abruptly when the automatic doors at the ER entrance didn't open fast enough. Speeding past the waiting area, she saw Barbara still on duty.

"Barbara." She caught a breath. "Mr. McGrath . . . the man I was talking to in the waiting room earlier this evening . . ."

The nurse raised one finger in a wait-a-second gesture and made a notation on the chart before her. Then she looked up.

"Cari, I'm so sorry about your friend." Barbara pushed back against the chair and sighed. "It's been one of those evenings!" She raised her eyes and shook her head. "But I did try to take him into the ER right away. The first time I came back to get him, he insisted I take a woman whose two-year-old was screaming loud enough to drown out rap music. Said his pain was going away. The next time I came for him, he was gone. One of the people in the waiting room said he'd gone to the rest room. We got busier and busier. You know how the ER is in the evening.

Colds and stomach flu and minor accidents. Two ambulances arrived with accident victims. By the time I got back to look for Mr. McGrath, I found him pale and perspiring and clutching his left arm. I rushed him to the cardiac room.''

Cari held her breath. ''How is he?''

Barbara's smile was as optimistic as her voice. ''He was stable when we transferred him to the ICU.'' She shuffled the papers before her, the smile slipping. ''Maybe if we had one side for colds and minor lacerations and another for emergencies, this wouldn't occur.'' She shook her head and gazed at Cari. ''But I did try to take him in to be examined twice.'' She gazed at Cari with no trace of a smile.

Cari nodded. No need to tell Barbara she might have acted differently. She probably wouldn't sleep half the night for worrying over it anyway. She, herself, had spent more than one sleepless night worrying over a patient. ''It happens.'' She made a wry face, raised a hand in parting, and strode from the room.

At the closed door to the intensive care unit, Cari paused to press the button on the intercom and requested to see Ben. An answering voice asked if she was a relative. Cari coughed and cleared her throat. It wasn't exactly a yes, but the door opened.

''Number four,'' a nurse said, not raising her gaze from the monitor before her.

Cari stepped into the glass-enclosed room and halted by Ben's bedside. She gazed at the elderly man tenderly and touched his hand.

Ben looked back, his gaze out of focus. ''Cari,'' he said groggily. ''Like my hotel room?''

''Not as well as I like your house.'' She kept her voice light.

''The doctor invited me, rather forcibly, to stay a few days. But don't worry. I'll be out of here before the next council meeting.''

Cari covered his hand with hers. ''I hope that's a promise. That microphone terrifies me.''

After leaving Ben, Cari stopped at the nurses' station, learning little more than she expected: the doctor would know more after the lab reports were returned in the morning.

Leaving the unit, Cari glanced into the waiting room to see if Ben's daughter, Margaret, had arrived. Half a dozen people sat in varying stages of unrest. Margaret wasn't among them. Cari turned and saw her approaching.

''Cari,'' Margaret said in an anxiety-laden voice. ''Where's ICU? Dad's . . . The nurse in the ER said Dad had been admitted to the ICU.''

''I know. I've just talked to him.''

''Is he okay?'' Margaret shook her head impatiently. ''That was a silly thing to ask. How could he be okay if he is in the intensive care unit?''

''He's stable,'' Cari said gently. ''That's our way of saying he's okay right now.''

''Right now?'' Margaret's voice trembled.

''Why don't you go in and see for yourself?'' Cari turned, waited for the distraught daughter to move, and retraced her steps to the intercom. Waiting for the nurse to answer, she turned to Margaret. ''He's groggy. The doctor ordered a pain medication.''

''Pain medication?''

"When Ben came in, he said he had a little pain in his arms from working with the roses."

"Those roses." Margaret sighed in anxious exasperation.

Cari smiled gently. "They are important to him." She paused, glancing at the silent intercom box. Everyone in the unit must be busy. She looked at Margaret as if the delay was normal. "By the time the nurse took Ben into the ER, his symptoms were more severe."

"Stroke . . . heart attack?" Margaret paled.

"Possibly a heart attack. The doctor will be more definite after he looks at the lab work in the morning."

The intercom crackled, emitting a voice seconds later. Cari leaned toward Margaret. "Tell the nurse you want to see Mr. McGrath and you are his daughter. She'll let you right in to see Ben if someone isn't working at the bedside."

Alarm clouded Margaret's eyes.

"Drawing blood for tests or changing his IV or just checking his vital signs." Cari touched Margaret's arm gently. "Ben was joking when I saw him. I think I got out of there just before he could ask me to see that his roses received a little TLC tonight."

"Can you go in with me?" Margaret asked shakily.

"The nurses only like one visitor at a time with the patient. I'll be in the waiting room."

Margaret looked embarrassed. "I'm so scared. My husband is in Los Angeles. I couldn't reach him." She moved to speak into the intercom, turning to Cari when the door didn't open. "It helps, you know, when he's here."

Cari nodded silently.

"He was with me when Mother went to the hospital. She died a few days later. He stayed with me." She glanced at the door as it opened, then back at Cari. "Will you wait for me?" At Cari's nod, she took a deep breath and walked inside.

Cari walked to the waiting room and filled a coffee cup before she found an empty chair. Involuntarily, she thought of Rand, her anger at him forgotten for the moment. He'd be the kind of husband who'd stay with you in a crisis.

The coffee was cold by the time Margaret returned. "The nurse said I should go home and she would call me if there was a significant change in his condition."

"That is a good idea. Ben may sleep all night and be waiting for you to visit tomorrow. You want to be rested enough to see him."

Margaret looked doubtful.

"That way, you can phone your husband early and tell him about Ben's condition before you come to the hospital. And you can call the unit tonight, or what's left of the night, and ask the nurse about Ben."

Margaret nodded. "I guess I should tell the nurse I'm going home."

"Yes." Cari endorsed the reluctant decision. She waited for Margaret to relay the information, and they walked out of the hospital together.

Cari left Hawthorne House early the next morning in order to visit Ben before she went to the operating room. She caught a fleeting glimpse of Rand as he went to another room for his first case, but to her relief, they didn't bump into each other in the crowded department.

She didn't see him Thursday or Friday. She told herself she was glad. So they hadn't parted all that amicably! It could be a good thing. She'd begun feeling too friendly toward him. She needed to remember his goal.

Friday afternoon, she made a casserole under Maggie's direction. Just because he was her rival didn't mean she had to renege on her word.

She slid the casserole dish in the oven. ''Did I tell you I'm going to San Francisco on Sunday to see my mother?'' She closed the oven door and turned to face her friend. ''If my car will make it. The engine keeps sputtering and hacking like it has asthma.''

''I thought you were on call this weekend.''

''Reba is taking Sunday call. Mom will only be in Frisco for the weekend. My stepfather has a band engagement.''

She shook her head at the offer of coffee. ''I've got a few things to do in case I get called out all day tomorrow. Maybe when I come back to take the casserole out of the oven.''

When Cari returned, Rand sat at the kitchen table sipping coffee with Mrs. Branson. Against her wishes, Cari's heartbeat quickened.

''Hi.'' Her voice was a little louder and a little more exuberant than she intended. What did one say after her outburst the last time she'd seen Rand? She walked to the oven, removed the dish, and placed it on a hot pad on the counter.

''Do you have time for coffee now?'' Maggie nodded to an empty cup on the table. ''I was telling Rand about the barbecue tomorrow.'' She turned back to Rand. ''Sometimes we do chicken or a roast on the rotisserie, but tomorrow evening everyone is bringing their own meat or chicken or whatever they prefer to put on the grill. My husband likes to cook, so you just tell him how you want it.''

''What else do I bring?''

Maggie looked at Cari. ''What are you bringing, dear?''

''Macaroni salad.'' Cari fiddled with the cup, hesitant to make a commitment to stay for coffee.

Maggie grinned at Rand. ''Everyone sort of checks in here so we don't have all salads and no desserts.''

Rand's grin included Cari. ''Macaroni salad sounds good.''

Cari nodded. It probably would be, since she was picking it up at the deli.

''How about French bread?'' Mrs. Branson suggested to Rand. ''Some of the supermarkets make it fresh daily, or you can pick it up at the deli already buttered and seasoned.''

''The bakery at the supermarket on Tenth Street makes it daily,'' Cari added. The market was blocks from her favorite deli and she didn't need to run into Rand any more than necessary.

Maggie looked at Rand. ''I'll make a jar of sun tea. If you want anything else to drink, you can bring it. Jolene is bringing dessert and green salad, and my husband will bake potatoes on the grill.'' She looked at Cari and lifted her cup for a refill.

Cari filled her cup as she refilled Maggie's and glared at her silent beeper. Why, when you wanted it to buzz, didn't the darn thing make a sound? Reluctantly, she sat down across from Rand, keeping her gaze focused on anything except the surgeon.

Maggie stirred her coffee, continuing to talk to Rand. ''You'll get to meet the Smiths and their four-year-old son, Joey. The Smiths are divorced and Joey is in nursery school about ten hours a day, so we only see him on weekends. It's so nice to have a young one around. Though his father takes up most of his time at the party. He gets Joey every other weekend. Since they both see so little of Joey, they agreed on sharing him at the barbecue.''

''Nice that parents can shelve their differences at times.'' Rand turned to Cari. ''Did you work today? I didn't see you.''

''I was assigned to a different room.''

''Not that the nurse in my room wasn't great, but I missed''—he cleared his throat—''your efficiency.''

''Thank you.'' Cari gulped her coffee and arose. ''I traded call with Reba tonight. I think I'll check in with the supervisor and see if any cases are pending.'' She left without looking at Rand. As she climbed the stairs, she remembered the casserole. She shrugged. Maggie would give it to him. Hopefully she wouldn't mention who had made it.

Cari worked at the hospital until eleven and was called out again at four in the morning. By six-thirty Saturday evening, she told herself she was too tired to attend the barbecue. Even if all she had to do was walk downstairs. She picked up the macaroni salad from the deli, transferred it to a plastic salad bowl, collected her silverware and plate, and went downstairs. Pausing before she closed her door, she wondered if Maggie had told Rand everyone brought their own utensils.

She decided it was wiser to take a second set than knock on Rand's door. He'd given no indication that he remembered her outburst. And she was glad she'd told him she was against selling Hawthorne House. Still, she felt uncomfortable. She returned to her cupboard.

Leaving the salad in the Bransons' refrigerator, Cari carried her dishes to the utility porch, pausing in the doorway to look at the people on the lattice-covered patio. Joey and his parents had arrived, and the Bransons were laughing at the preschooler's performance on a toy horn. Joey's parents shared a smile, which wasn't their usual behavior toward each other.

Cari found the gaiety infectious and scanned the yard for Rand. She didn't see him, and her smile slipped. She trudged down the ramp, pausing to glance at the upstairs windows. Even if Maggie hadn't mentioned the time, Joey's horn was like an alarm clock.

Cari placed her dishes on a table, smiling weakly at the others without interrupting the young performer. Rand could be at the hospital. Involuntarily, she realized the sudden droop in her spirits was more from disappointment than weariness. Which was confusing. Hadn't she been trying to avoid him?

Chapter Six

Even more confusing was the way her heart soared when Rand strolled down the ramp to the patio. He balanced two loaves of bread and two carriers of wine cooler, and Cari thought he looked a little hesitant about joining the others.

Dressed in a short-sleeve shirt and khaki trousers, his casual attire differed from the scrubs or sports-coat-and-pant ensembles he usually wore to the hospital. Cari dipped her head, busying her hands with smoothing the plastic tablecloth. While Maggie Branson introduced Rand to Joey's parents, Jolene and Kent Smith, she secured a corner of the plastic that had flipped up in the late afternoon breeze. Another breeze, carrying the scent of roses from Ben's yard, caught the tendrils of her hair and scattered them across her forehead. She brushed them aside and looked up. Rand stood as if listening to Joey's father, but his gaze moved across the expanse, pausing when it reached hers. Her fingers stilled, immobilized under the spell of his gaze. Flecks of silver brightened the warm, green irises of his eyes, as if the setting sun had flung a spray of silver dust across the patio.

Cari smiled, mouthing a ''welcome to the party.''

His lips curved in acknowledgment and he pulled his gaze away, as if reluctant to return his attention to the speaker. Cari repositioned the knives and forks beside the plates, dropping a fork and using it as an excuse to escape to the kitchen. She moved to speak to John on the way, asking if the coals were ready for her to bring the food for the grill. The cook shook his head, scanning the burning briquettes as if he could test the temperature with his eyesight. Cari turned away to skip up the ramp and through the cluttered utility porch to the kitchen. She rinsed the fork, then turned the faucet handle to cold and let the cool water wash over her hands. She dried the fork and knew if she dallied longer, she'd be missed.

When she returned, Rand was offering wine coolers to the guests. He paused before Cari, the warm eyes still sparkling.

Cari shook her head. "I'll take a rain check. I'm on call."

"Ah, we need to synchronize our schedules. Jim's on call for our group this weekend."

The scent of his soap and shaving lotion wafted around Cari as she turned the fork in her fingers. "I hope he doesn't get called for a patient who needs surgery in the next few hours. I'm looking forward to a well-grilled chicken breast and Jolene's dessert."

"I'm partial to desserts myself. What's the treat this evening? Or is that supposed to remain a surprise?" His head dipped forward, his gaze meeting hers humorously.

He stood far too close, blocking out the other occupants of the patio. Even Joey's laughter seemed far away. "It's going to be a surprise to me, but Jolene does come up with some interesting desserts. She likes to watch the cooking shows when she's home.''

''Which doesn't seem often. This is the first time I've seen her.''

''I think she spent last weekend with her parents.'' Vaguely, she heard the sound of her name and realized it was the second time she'd heard it. Embarrassed, she turned to look toward the grill.

''I think the coals are ready,'' John called jovially.

Cari nodded and grinned at Rand. ''Duty beckons.'' She moved hurriedly away to set the fork down before she went to the kitchen. Inside, she paused and caught her breath. Despite the enclosed room, it felt cooler than the patio.

For a moment.

Then Rand stepped through the open door. ''Need some help?'' he asked brightly.

Cari opened the refrigerator door, trying to think of some witty remark to send him back to the patio. But her tongue was as unnerved as her hands. She withdrew the packages Maggie had marked. ''You could carry the dessert to the patio while I unwrap this stuff and put it on a tray.''

When Rand returned, Cari handed him the loaded tray to take to John. She didn't meet his eyes. ''I'll bring the salads.''

When she placed the salad dishes on the table, she saw Rand tossing a ball to Joey. She poured a glass of iced tea and moved toward Maggie. The older woman smiled and motioned to a nearby chair, and the spongy rubber ball plopped on the concrete near her as she sat down. She leaned over to catch the errant ball and felt Rand's fingers close over hers.

Fingers tingling, Cari released the ball, leaned back in her chair, and laughed shakily as Rand continued to stand beside her.

"It's easy to see you like children," Maggie said.

Rand chuckled. "I have three nephews, two nieces, and one whose gender my younger sister is keeping a secret. Yes, I like children." He grinned at Joey to stay his impatience. "Sad to say, I can't see any of my own in my future until I establish my practice."

"Is it going well?" Maggie asked.

"Fine. I wanted to specialize in pediatric orthopedics, but Jim and I decided Buena Vista needs another general orthopedist. Fortunately for me, I see a number of children in a day's work." He grinned apologetically at Joey's insistent beckoning and moved away to toss the oversize sponge ball to the youngster.

Cari glanced across the patio. Joey's parents, unusually, were absorbed in conversation.

"I miss Reba and Ben and the Greens," Maggie said. "It seems more festive when everyone is here."

"Where are the Greens this evening?"

"Didn't I tell you? They've gone on one of those bus tours. Plan to be gone three weeks."

"Sounds nice." Cari felt her gaze slipping away to watch Rand toss the bright yellow ball to the toddler.

Maggie slid her hand over Cari's. "He'll make a good father for some lucky girl's children."

"No doubt there is more than one female employee at the hospital who would agree with you."

"Don't you?"

"Of course. I just meant they're interested."

"You aren't?"

Cari forced a laugh. ''You know I'm allergic to marriage. Something in my genes, I think.''

''Pshaw! Just because your parents failed doesn't mean you have to.''

''You haven't heard about apples that don't fall far from the tree?''

''I've heard that persistence is a powerful ally.'' Maggie's tone was teasing.

Cari returned the grin, her tone equally teasing. ''My whole stockpile of persistence is allocated to saving Hawthorne House right now. And the man you're pointing out to me is the opposition. Does that sound like a recipe for romance?''

''Love could find a way.''

Cari giggled. ''What romance author is writing your dialogue this week?''

Maggie chuckled. ''Cari, you know what I mean.''

Cari lifted her eyebrows in feigned awe. But she avoided looking at Rand for fear her eyes would betray her. Just seeing him with Joey made her wish for a wonderful marriage to a loving husband and, to make it complete, a couple of children. Her inner voice laughed wickedly. A lasting marriage was as out of date as a Victorian household. Did she want her children left with a baby-sitter while she worked double shifts to support them? She sighed silently, staring into the distance. She wanted the whole ten yards. The husband, the children, the home, and the storybook ending.

She reached for the glass she'd placed on the wobbly table between her and Maggie and took a swallow of tea, letting the liquid cool her mind as well as her throat. A thought like that mustn't find a home in her head, let alone her heart. No matter how attractive and unnerving Rand was, his clinic would destroy the security and happiness she'd found in her grandmother's house.

Rand tossed the ball to Joey, but his gaze followed Cari. He admired the way she looked in her colorful T-shirt and walking shorts. She was only rearranging the food, but he had to force himself to look away to catch an incoming ball. When he looked back, the late afternoon breeze tossed her hair playfully around her face as she adjusted the weights on the plastic tablecloth to keep it from blowing askew.

He'd been a little hesitant to join the people on the patio. Not only because his social life had been stagnant for a long time, but because he would be responsible for uprooting these people from their home. From their barbecue parties, from their camaraderie and closeness. His family had had barbecues when he was younger. While he was overseas, he'd missed the warmth and closeness of family and friends laughing over a hodgepodge of food spread across picnic tables, as these people were doing. And he was going to destroy this house. And with it any chance of gaining Cari Masterson's affection.

He'd been surprised to find Cari was the one who didn't want to sell. It pained him to think he was in conflict with her. But he was too far into the construction of the clinic to back out. He was obligated to his partner, his father, even his sisters who had agreed with their father about selling the land and loaning the money to Rand. Decisions about the property couldn't be made by him alone now. Even if he wanted to bail out to appease Cari, he couldn't assure her Hawthorne House would remain sitting unscathed on Oak Street any more than he could stop thinking about its lovely owner.

There was nothing he could do about it. He was committed to buying the house, if possible, and building the clinic on the site. He strode back to his game position. ''Ready, Joey?''

The youngster nodded eagerly, and the two resumed their game. His thoughts resumed their tumbling. Even if Cari could forgive him for demolishing the house, to pursue her would be folly. With his responsibilities at the moment, he had little time to do more than think about marriage. The clinic and starting a new practice would claim all his waking hours. Bad timing for a successful marriage. He tossed the ball to Joey and his gaze wandered again, locating Cari near Maggie Branson. She turned, those lovely animated eyes sparkling beneath well-shaped eyebrows, and looked his way.

He almost missed the ball again as she walked toward him.

''John forgot to ask how you want your meat cooked.''

Food was not the subject on his mind, but Rand managed to reply without stuttering. ''Brown on the outside, pink on the inside.''

Cari grinned. ''That sounds nicer than medium rare.''

''My dad orders his by saying 'pass it over the fire, but don't let it stop to chat.' ''

''Your dad sounds like a fun guy.''

''I never thought of him as any different from other fathers.''

''Fathers aren't all the same.'' Cari's smile didn't waver. ''I should know. I've had four.''

Rand lifted his eyebrows in awe, suppressing his awareness of the hint of pain in her voice.

Her forehead wrinkled humorously. ''At the last count.''

Rand grinned. Her humor was infectious. ''Since I've had only one, I bow to your voice of experience.''

She chuckled wryly. ''It wouldn't have been my chosen field in which to gain experience.'' She cocked her head reflectively. ''My stepfathers were okay. Even though they didn't stay around long enough for me to learn their good points.'' She shifted her gaze momentarily to acknowledge Joey's approach. She asked him about school and if his grandfather had had any new lambs when he'd visited him.

Rand's heart warmed. She liked children too. She was good with them. He barely had time to conceal his rising admiration with a quick blink when he saw her turning back to him.

''Time to put in your order before John charcoals the steak.''

Rand watched her as she walked away, aware of Joey tugging at the leg of his pants. He liked her sense of humor. And her sense of caring, even away from her professional duties. He'd noticed her checking to see if Maggie needed her tea glass refilled before she sat down.

He gave the ball to Joey and motioned for him to toss it. He knew Cari stopped to visit the wheelchair-bound lady after work. Most people wanted to kick off their shoes and plop in front of the TV. But not Cari, from what he'd seen. She changed her clothes and went to work on the paint job on the front of the house.

She was the kind of woman he wanted to marry.

Either the shock of the realization or his inattention to the yellow ball sent it past his open hands. He strode across the patio following it.

The thought didn't disappear. It bounced in his head like the ball bouncing across the patio. She was not only the kind of girl he wanted to marry, she was *the* girl he wanted to marry. He retrieved the ball and straightened his tall frame. But that would be impossible. Of all the people here today who'd view him with loathing when the house came tumbling down, Cari Masterson would hate him most of all.

A sound from her beeper alerted Cari as she carried Maggie's food to the table. She placed the plate on the table, and Maggie grinned sympathetically.

''I hear your phone ringing.''

Cari lifted one hand in resignation. ''Tell John to leave my chicken on the grill. I'll be back in a minute.''

But it was near ten o'clock when she returned to Hawthorne House.

She entered the dim hallway, glancing longingly toward the rear hall where it led to the utility porch and the patio. She walked down the hall and onto the porch, knowing the patio would be dark and the embers in the grill dying. She'd so hoped the others might have lingered to chat that she hadn't even detoured to go through a fast-food place when her stomach reminded her it was far past dinnertime.

She trudged up the stairs with mixed emotions. She

hadn't minded going to the hospital. She liked her work. She knew she wasn't the one saving a life, but the operating surgeon and anesthetist needed her assistance. She felt satisfaction.

Inside her apartment, she opened the refrigerator and scanned the meager contents before closing the door. She opened a cupboard and eyed a box of cereal balefully. She wouldn't starve. Pulling the cereal box from the shelf, she placed it on the table and went to the bedroom to get a towel and robe. Dinner could wait until she'd showered.

Rand was waiting in his doorway when she returned. "I missed you at dinner."

A rush of pleasure sent a smile to her lips. "I was playing nurse in the OR."

"Maggie told us you'd been called to the hospital when you didn't return. Did you have any dinner?"

"Not even a chocolate bar from the snack cart."

"That's good. I wouldn't want the fabulous dinner I saved for you to go to the Bransons' cat." He tried to look serious, but his eyes sparkled. "I'll take it out of the fridge if you'll wait a minute."

He returned seconds later, balancing three dishes, and gazed at the towel and clothes in her hands. "On second thought, I'll pop the chicken in the microwave while you're hanging up your things."

Cari clutched the damp towel and fled to her bedroom. Her glance spun away from the mirror over her dresser. How could actresses achieve that glamorous look in a terry cloth turban when her towel-wrapped tresses made her look like a lost member of a street sect?

Discarding the towel in favor of a blow-dryer, she

rearranged her hair. By the time she'd darkened her eyelashes and brightened her lips, she decided she looked presentable. Even slightly attractive.

She ignored a momentary warning that the man she'd donned the lipstick for was the man bent on destroying her home. She concentrated on calming the chaos in her chest.

The small, round table was set with her dinnerware, and Rand stood before the microwave removing dishes. He turned as if he sensed her presence.

''Your timing is right on.'' He placed the dishes on the counter and moved behind a chair. ''Is this table all right, Miss?''

She laughed, going along with his charade. ''What did I do to rate the best table in the house?''

''Smiled at the right people.'' He draped a tea towel over his left arm and reached for a bottle of wine cooler. Opening it, he poured a couple of ounces into the water glass by Cari's plate. ''I hope you'll find this satisfactory.'' He waited patiently for her to lift the glass.

Cari's grin widened.

''I'm sorry. Our shipment of wineglasses didn't come in today, but I don't think it will change the taste.''

Cari lifted the glass. A sip wouldn't hurt, and she didn't want to destroy the mood.

With a satisfied smile, Rand stepped back into the tiny kitchen and returned with the warmed dishes. Arranging them on the table, he stood back. ''Will there be anything else?'' He struggled to keep his face straight.

Cari's heart skipped a beat. She didn't want him to

go. She didn't want this moment to end. "Yes." It was her turn to keep a straight face. "Will you join me? Share my wine? Have a cup of coffee?"

He hesitated.

"You left something cooking in your toaster oven?" Her voice was teasing.

"No."

"I have instant coffee." She stood up.

"Sit down. I'll share your wine, and I know where the glasses are."

Warmth spread through Cari. She couldn't recall when anyone other than a waiter had served her. It gave her a nice feeling.

Cari cut a thin slice of meat from the rewarmed chicken breast. "Did you enjoy the barbecue?"

"I did." He looked at the meat on her fork. "I'm waiting to see if you like your chicken." He eyed the food again. "Eat. Your body needs refueling."

"Medical advice from a waiter? Or did you change hats?"

"I change hats easily." He took a sip of wine. "When I was overseas, I delivered a baby one minute and cooked dinner for the other children the next." He grinned sheepishly at Cari's smile of admiration. "There was no one else to do it, and the kids were hungry."

Cari lifted a slice of meat to her mouth. Modest, too. For a doctor, he didn't cease to surprise her. She swallowed, forcing her thoughts to the food, and managed a smile of satisfaction. "I'll have to tell John that chicken is better rewarmed."

"Praise like that makes it worth slaving over a cold microwave oven."

''Do you do dishes too?''

''About as often as I deliver babies. Only in an emergency or if the paper plate plant is on strike.''

''So tell me about your medical practice in a third-world country.'' Cari took a bite of Jolene's cake without tasting it. Despite not having eaten since breakfast, food wasn't a priority. Keeping Rand talking was. She liked to watch his lips as he spoke. She liked to see the animation in his eyes when he talked about medicine.

It was near midnight when Rand stood and carried the dishes to the sink in the tiny kitchen. Seconds later, Cari heard water running.

She stood up, carrying her plate to the counter. ''I thought you didn't do dishes.''

''Rinsing them isn't washing them.'' He reached for the plate and his eyes met hers.

She knew she should relinquish the dish and step away. But her fingers clutched the ceramic as if they'd been doused with glue. Her gaze was equally unresponsive. She couldn't pull it away from Rand's magnetic look.

She felt the dish move from her fingers and saw Rand place it in the sink with one hand. With the other hand, he held her fingers firmly. Her heartbeat quickened. ''One thing about this kitchen, it's difficult for two people to work without bumping into each other.'' She was embarrassed by the tremulous note in her voice.

Without releasing her fingers, he turned slowly to face her. ''Not a bad way to build a kitchen.'' His other hand slipped around her waist.

Cari laughed nervously. ''I like the kitchen downstairs. Roomy enough for a table so the family can kibitz while Mom is baking cookies.''

''I like the kitchen upstairs. A man wouldn't have to run far to catch his woman.'' His left hand released her fingers and slipped to her waist. His right hand rose to slip a tress of hair behind her ear.

Cari caught her breath and smelled the scent of the wine he'd tasted. His breath was soft and warm and seemed to reach out and fan her lips. She knew she should laugh now and tell him she needed to get some sleep in case she was called out to the OR again. But her feet wouldn't move.

It could be the wine. It could be that she'd had a long day. Or it could be that she was falling in love. The thought gave her the strength to raise one hand and place it against his chest. But before she could push away, he'd captured the hand, lowered it to his waist, and returned his hand to touch her back.

''Now what were we talking about?''

''Kitchens?'' She tried to recall that this man planned to demolish her kitchen, but her brain didn't activate readily.

''Kitchens. I seem to recall you like large ones and I like small ones.'' His forefinger trailed down her cheek with seductive lethargy.

''But you like children. Would you deprive them of room to help bake cookies?''

''Maybe I'll have two kitchens in my house.'' He pulled her closer, his breath fanning her ear.

Cari breathed carefully. Through the thin layer of terry cloth, his chest felt firm and strong. She wanted to relax against the masculine frame, wanted to forget that marriage was not part of her future plans. Her fingers tightened on his waist, letting the warmth of his skin through the thin cotton shirt radiate through her fingers. Why couldn't she pretend that marriages lasted forever? For a little while? What harm could it do if it was only pretense? If she firmly kept in mind that Rand could not be a part of her life? She wanted to be kissed and held and made to feel special. At the moment, standing in the circle of his arms in the tiny kitchenette, that feeling seemed more important than Gran's legacy.

She lifted her head, aware it was an invitation.

The invitation wasn't ignored. Rand pulled her closer, as his head dipped and his eyes captured hers with an intense gaze that softened quickly. His lips touched hers, soft as a moth's wing. They moved to tease her earlobe, her neck, her cheek, and returned to savor her lips.

Cari had never been kissed like this. A fleeting thought in the back of her mind told her any pretense was worth this feeling.

She wasn't hurting anyone. Especially Rand. Hadn't he said he couldn't marry until his practice was successful?

He released her reluctantly and she pulled her head back. ''I didn't mean to interrupt your work.'' Her voice sounded breathless, and a little scared, to her.

''This is one interruption any dish rinser would enjoy.''

Cari laughed uneasily. ''It's late, and I'm still on call.''

Rand nodded. ''I think you can finish these.'' He dried his hands on a towel and turned to go.

''Rand.'' Cari couldn't stop the word, but she

dipped her head. No doubt her eyes were glowing like home fires, and that wouldn't do. "I . . . I just wanted to thank you for dinner. It was wonderful."

"My pleasure." His deep voice emphasized the words.

After he left, Cari locked the door and went to bed. An hour later, she was still awake. She couldn't lock a door against thoughts of the green-eyed doctor.

Chapter Seven

The radio alarm woke Cari at seven. She opened her eyes slowly. Reba had taken call for her; she'd only set the alarm in order to have time to visit Ben at the hospital before she left for San Francisco.

Her next thought was of Rand. Handsome, thoughtful, caring, modest Rand. Perilous thoughts. She sat up and swung her feet to the floor. A few kisses didn't change anything. He still planned to erect a clinic on the ruins of her home.

Strangely, the morbid thought didn't keep her from humming as she plopped a piece of whole wheat bread in the toaster half an hour later. Nor stopping, toast in hand, to gaze at the closed door across from hers with a foolish smile before she skipped down the stairs.

On the drive to the hospital, her car coughed and wheezed like an asthmatic romping in a hay field, but she scarcely noticed. A line from a long forgotten song jogged through Cari's head, and she opened her mouth and sang three lines before she glanced guiltily at a passing car. Abruptly, she concluded her solo. It was the morning sun that produced this irrational cheerfulness, she decided. A frown would disintegrate under the warmth and light radiating from the glittering disk overhead.

The sensation didn't evaporate as she stepped from beneath the sun's rays to the neon-lit interior of the hospital. She floated down the hospital corridors, automatically scanning the intersecting hallways and nurses' stations before reaching the closed door of the intensive care unit. She paused before pressing the intercom button. Behind her, the sound of voices floated down the hallway and she turned to gaze toward the intersecting hallway. A nurse dressed in a colorful tunic and white pants and a doctor dangling a stethoscope from one hand strode past without looking her way. Cari blushed, realizing she'd hoped to see Rand. Even worse, she acknowledged she'd looked down every hall on the way to the unit in search of his familiar figure.

Shaking her head at her irrational behavior, Cari pressed the intercom and identified herself. Seconds later, a mumbled reply informed her Ben had been transferred to a medical unit. Her smile returned. Ben's condition had improved enough to merit his move out of the ICU. She turned with lightened steps, ignoring the intruding thought that Rand seldom had patients on the medical floor.

Approaching the room to which Ben had been transferred, she paused at the sight of Ben's daughter.

"Good morning, Margaret," she said cheerfully. "I thought only doctors and nurses visited the hospital this early on Sunday."

Margaret grinned sheepishly. "I was worried that he wouldn't adjust to floor care. In the special unit he barely lifted a hand before someone was at his bedside."

Cari nodded. "I know. Sometimes patients do think

they're getting less attention when they are transferred out of the unit, but it's because they don't need the same level of care. Ben doesn't need one-on-one care any longer or the doctor wouldn't have taken him out of the unit.'' She smiled, trying to relay her confidence to Margaret. ''The nurses on this floor are excellent. I've worked with some of them.''

Margaret returned the smile tentatively. ''He is better. Improving, as you medical people say. His health, I mean, not his spirits. I told him his room would be ready at our house when he is discharged from the hospital, and he looked at me like I was a stranger.'' She lowered her gaze to stare at the tiled flooring. ''The doctor suggested it,'' she added, as if an explanation was necessary. ''I'm not forcing him to sell the house and move in with us. I want to take care of him.'' Tears brimmed in her eyes as she raised her eyelids. ''I know he doesn't want to leave his roses. Or maybe it's his way of retaining his independence. Not that I blame him.'' She paused and took a deep breath. ''But I can't stop worrying.'' She blinked rapidly. ''We had a guest room built for him last year. He'd have his own entrance.'' She shook her head morosely. ''I hate to leave him looking so gloomy, but I think my presence just adds to his unhappiness.''

Cari gave Margaret a sympathetic look. ''I was on my way to visit him. I'll tell him his roses are bursting out all over. That should get a grin at least. I'll even tell him I'm keeping an eye on them.''

''Thanks,'' Margaret said. She raised a hand in parting and turned to walk slowly down the hall.

Cari proceeded to Ben's room. Curtains hanging from ceiling tracks enclosed the bed on the far side of the two-patient room. Cari paused outside the draped partition. Below the drapes, she could see two white-trousered legs and white shoes.

"Hi," she said, facing the curtain. "Could I come in and say hello to Ben? I'll only stay a minute."

"Of course," a pleasant voice replied.

Cari stepped around the enclosure and found an opening. A young nursing assistant Cari didn't recognize draped a towel over Ben's bare chest and straightened the bath blanket over his lower extremities.

"What's this?" Cari teased. "A bed bath? You look well enough to be up and watering your roses."

Life filtered into Ben's dull eyes. "That's what I told this nurse. She must have sick people to care for, but she just keeps hanging around." He grinned with weak wickedness at the young nurse. "Probably my charming personality. That's what one of the ICU nurses said."

"I wouldn't dispute that," Cari said. She glanced at the nursing assistant, aware the aide had a schedule. She turned back to Ben. "I just wanted to teli you the roses are fine. I'll check on them again when I get back from San Francisco this evening."

"San Francisco?" A faint sparkle beamed in Ben's eyes. "A new beau?"

"Would I go out with someone new just because you're holding hands with another woman?" She rolled her eyes at Ben and turned slightly to grin at the nurse. "My stepfather finally has a show in San Francisco," she continued, "so I'm going to visit my mom."

''Good,'' Ben said. ''It's time she returned to California. Will they be here long?''

''The show was last night and they're leaving for Tahoe tonight.''

''Look on the bright side,'' Ben quipped weakly. ''They could be out of work and moving in with you.''

Cari laughed. ''Yeah. My place is so roomy.''

''But it's yours.''

Cari's fingers tightened on her handbag, kneading the soft leather. ''At the moment.'' Her voice was solemn.

''Hey,''—Ben lifted a shaky hand, turning a palm out—''we'll beat 'em. I'll be out of the hospital and storming the gates of the City Council by the next meeting.''

Cari's smile felt as weak as the limp hand Ben waved. ''Not if I don't let the nurses get on with your treatments.'' She added emphasis to the words by waving and skipping around the curtain. Outside the room, she took a breath. She should have gone into show business instead of nursing. The brightness in her voice had been superb acting.

She had depended on Ben for support in her campaign to keep Hawthorne House. For her, speaking at a council meeting was on a par with entering an arena filled with hostile lions.

She turned toward the stairs leading to the operating room. Maybe Ben would be up and able to attend the meeting. With him cheering her on, she might even approach the microphone without having an attack of paralysis. Meanwhile, if Reba was working, she wanted to thank her again for taking call.

She stopped outside the sterile area when she saw

her friend at a distance, with a load of soiled linen. ''Morning, Reba. I see you're working.''

''Helping clean up after an appy.'' Reba crammed the sheets and towels into the color-coded hamper reserved for nondisposable covers. ''We have another case to go in an hour. An accident case. Dr. Barstow's.'' She rolled the hamper aside. ''Come and have a fast cup of coffee with me.'' She motioned toward the chairs by the desk.

Cari hesitated. She had to allow for the time it would take to coax and coddle her car to San Francisco, considering the asthmatic condition of the engine this morning. Still, she wasn't in all that big a rush. ''Sounds good.'' She walked to the coffee maker.

Shaking a packet of sugar into one cup, she stirred the mixture and handed it to Reba. ''How are you doing with the physical therapist?''

Reba took a sip of the liquid before she tilted her head and lifted her eyes merrily. ''He's taking me to breakfast after the next case.''

''Someplace romantic like the hospital dining room, no doubt.'' Cari teased.

''Even McDonald's glows with candles and soft music when I'm with Greg,'' Reba said glibly.

''Ah, love,'' Cari crooned.

''Don't knock it 'til you try it.'' Reba laughed. ''Which reminds me, Dr. Carson was here a while ago. Asked if you'd been by.''

Cari rolled her eyes and shook her head. Reba was a hopeless romantic. With hopeless being the key word where Cari was concerned. Hopeless, she repeated firmly, determined to ignore the flutter of butterflies in her chest. "Did he mention the barbecue?"

"He said he'd had a great time but you were called away on a case." Reba turned away in answer to a ring from the telephone. Lifting the receiver, she grinned wickedly at Cari. "I'll bet he was disappointed that you had to leave, even if he didn't say so. He said they'd saved dinner for you."

Feeling a flush of heat rise in her throat, Cari was relieved to see Reba's attention turn to the telephone. She pressed her fingers against the cool surface beneath her right hand. Rand wouldn't have mentioned he'd waited up for her, the least of what he'd done. Saved her dinner, served her food, and kissed her soundly!

Cari had finished her coffee by the time the telephone conversation was over. She heard the door to the doctors' lounge open. "That's probably Dr. Barstow checking to see if you're ready," she said softly. She placed her cup on a tray destined for the dishwasher. "I should get on the road anyway. The sound my car is making means I'm not going to push it too fast. I just hope I don't have to have it towed home."

"You won't," a familiar voice said nearby, "if you leave it at home."

"Leave it at home?" Cari repeated. She turned to acknowledge the speaker, and the butterflies lounging near her lungs decided to practice some kind of rain dance that interfered with her breathing.

Embarrassed, she glanced to see if Reba had noticed, but Reba was reaching to answer the telephone again. "And how do I get to San Francisco? Jog?" she managed to ask merrily. Maybe acting was in her blood. Hadn't her father been in the entertainment business?

"You could ride with me." Rand leaned one hip against the lengthy desk. "Maggie mentioned your car is ailing. She would never forgive me if your car broke down and you were stranded when I'm going to San Francisco today."

"You just happen to be going to San Francisco?"

Rand nodded. "It was either take Jim's call, or drive his father-in-law to the airport. I need a break."

Cari's migratory talent for acting deserted her. "What time are you leaving?" she stammered.

Maggie was playing cupid, of course. Rand seemed no more eager to take her to Frisco than she was to go with him. It wasn't the journey to the city that worried her. It was the ride back. She wasn't ready to cope with any time alone with Rand. Not after last night. She had to stay at arm's length where Rand was concerned. She was attracted to him more than she wanted to be. From his voice right now, he didn't share the same feeling, or memories of last evening, that she had. He'd probably kissed her because she was within kissing distance. "I'd planned to have lunch with Mom. If that isn't convenient for you . . ." She let the words hang.

"I think we can work things out. The flight leaves a little after one. If we left at ten, I could drop you off before I took Jim's father-in-law to San Francisco International. Depending on the traffic, we could get there in plenty of time for Earl to check in."

Cari nodded slowly. The offer was a godsend—in one way. On the other hand, it was unnerving.

*   *   *

Cari found the drive to San Francisco pleasant. She enjoyed the cheerful three-way conversation. Even the mention of the clinic didn't unsettle her.

Near noon, Rand slowed in front of the hotel Cari had named, and Cari raised an eyebrow. Her stepfather's finances must be in good shape. Valet parking and bellmen at the curb. The last place she'd visited them, she'd helped carry luggage around the block and up a flight of stairs.

She picked up the jacket matching the cinnamon-colored walking shorts she'd worn, looped her over-size handbag on one arm, and reached for the door handle. The door swung open before she touched it, and Rand extended a hand.

Pausing to speak to the parking attendant, Rand walked with Cari to the lobby.

''Shall I wait until you are sure this is the right place and your mother is in?''

Cari smiled, pleased at his concern. She shook her head. ''This is the right hotel and I talked to Mom last night. She'll be in.''

Rand nodded. ''If you say so.'' He hesitated as if reluctant to leave her. ''Depending on traffic, it will take about an hour to drive to the airport. An hour back. What time shall I pick you up.''

''Mom is leaving at four. The wife of another band member is picking her up to drive to Tahoe. If you get back by three, you could meet her.'' This time, she hesitated. ''Maybe we could have coffee or something together.''

''I'd like that. What room shall I call?''

''You can't call her room.'' She made a face. ''I mean, Mom said she'd probably have to check out of

the hotel around noon and leave her luggage with the
bell captain. So we'd planned to have lunch and go
window-shopping. We could be back in the lobby
around three.'' She looked at him expectantly. She
wasn't sure she wanted him to say yes. Unlike Reba,
she wasn't ready to take anyone home to meet her
parents.

''Three might be optimistic if the traffic is anything
like the last time I drove in San Francisco. But I'll try
my best.''

Cari pulled her gaze from the lobby and focused it
on her watch. It was after four. She'd enjoyed lunch
and window shopping and talking. Not that her mother
had changed. Cari had elaborated on the frequent mis-
haps at Hawthorne House and her mother had recalled
similar disasters in places where they'd lived. Through
shared laughter and fleeting nostalgia, Cari felt they'd
become closer.

They'd returned to the hotel at three-thirty, but Rand
wasn't there and her mother had to leave. Between
scanning the lobby every few minutes, Cari reasoned
Rand was probably caught in a traffic jam. No cause
to panic.

Then she saw him stride through the entrance, his
hair ruffled in an appealing way. He carried a light
jacket haphazardly, as if he'd reached for it hurriedly
and slung it over his arm. The tension eased and a
smile softened her lips and her heart picked up a beat.

''Sorry I'm late,'' he said.

Cari's smile broadened. She was glad he'd spoken
before she could blurt out how glad she was to see
him.

''Traffic?''

Rand nodded, glancing around. ''Has your mother left?''

''Her friend picked her up a little while ago. Driving one of those mini–motor homes. Said they liked it better than living in hotels.''

''No room service.'' He stood catching his breath, his gaze focused on Cari. ''Outside of that, a motor home might be preferable to changing beds every few days.''

Cari laughed lightly, feeling warm and cheery for some reason. ''Mom's friend said something like that. I think she was trying to sell Mom and my stepfather on the idea of buying one so they could stay together in the campground.''

''Did she?''

''Mom likes room service. Even when they can't afford it,'' Cari said wryly.

''Did you have a good time?''

''We did.'' She nodded as if to emphasize the words, finding herself seeking Rand's gaze as if it was magnetized. To break the spell, she stood and lifted one hand. ''I imagine a cup of coffee sounds good about this time.''

''It does.''

''There is a coffee shop here. Or we could go somewhere else.''

Rand raised his eyelashes and scanned the area quickly, his glance flitting past the pots of yellow chrysanthemums decorating the planters and a sculpture surrounded by greenery. ''It is nice, but I'd like to walk a little.''

''I know. You've been driving most of the day.''

Cari straightened her jacket, picked up her purse, grateful for the necessity to move. She felt like an idiot. She couldn't stop looking at Rand, and she couldn't seem to mouth more than a few inane words at a time. It was as though the romantic city by the bay had cast a golden spell over her. Which was impossible. Just because they were alone in a different city didn't change his objective in Buena Vista. Or hers.

She focused on walking until they exited the hotel and stood on the sidewalk. She didn't glance at Rand. "Which way?" So far, the air hadn't increased her vocabulary, she noted.

Rand looked left and right. "Either way." His conversational skills seemed no better than hers. But he turned to the right. At the corner of the hotel, he turned again.

A light breeze touched Cari's cheeks, bringing the scent of the sea on the moist, salt-laden air.

Beyond the building, cocky white-and-gray gulls strutted among smaller gray pigeons on the red-tiled square. They turned onto a larger square and Cari felt Rand's fingers touch her arm, alerting her even before she became aware of the sound of wheels on the concrete surface. Despite the cool air, Cari felt a glow at the small protective gesture as a teenager on a skateboard whizzed by.

Rand removed his fingers. "I haven't had lunch yet, so we could combine coffee with an early dinner. Maybe Fisherman's Wharf. Or if Fisherman's Wharf doesn't appeal to you, there's Ghirardelli Square or Pier 39."

The tourist attractions of San Francisco. The sites

that advertised dining, with couples engrossed in each other while sipping wine against the magnificent backdrop of a shimmering sea or the Golden Gate Bridge. Or the city itself with its tall buildings and historic towers. Cari drew a calming breath. She hadn't planned on a romantic evening. Hamburgers at a drive-thru on the way back to Buena Vista sounded safe.

''You sound like you know the area.''

''I grew up in northern California. It was a big deal to drive to San Francisco for special occasions.''

Jealousy, so fleeting it left only a pinpoint of pain, stabbed Cari. Growing up in northern California, why wouldn't Rand take his dates to San Francisco?

''I'll flag a taxi.''

Cari watched Rand step toward the curb and raise a hand. He turned to give her an endearing grin when two taxis passed, then renewed his efforts to catch a driver's eye. Laughter bubbled in her heart. Why shouldn't she see Fisherman's Wharf or the other places? For one evening, she could pretend she was half of a romantic couple, each gazing enraptured into the other's eyes or viewing the scenic wonders. The memories of the sea and the ships and the span of bridges wouldn't keep her warm on a frosty night, but they would be wonderful memories. She didn't have that many.

When the third taxi passed, Cari stepped forward and touched Rand's arm. ''Mom said she'd taken a cable car to Fisherman's Wharf. Couldn't we ride one?''

Rand nodded. ''We have to walk a way to find a

boarding place, then walk to Fisherman's Wharf after we get off. Sure you want to do that?''

''I don't mind.'' For some inexplicable reason, right now she could walk to the moon, or at least halfway, with Rand beside her. *Which is not the way I should feel,* Cari scolded herself. *This is not a date. Rand is showing me Fisherman's Wharf because he's hungry and we might as well eat there as anywhere. It's another indication of his thoughtfulness.*

At the sight of yellow lines on the street, Rand paused and indicated this was a boarding area. The car stopped, and Cari boarded with a sense of excitement and adventure. It was only a cable car, she told herself. A little different kind of transportation. But it seemed like more to Cari. Maybe it was the history surrounding it—Rand had said the car line started in the eighteen hundreds; with a renovation in 1982, it was still running well. Or maybe it was a combination of the cable cars, their history, and being in San Francisco with Rand. Most of all, being with Rand. A warning, fleeting as a jet trail, reminded her of their different goals regarding Hawthorne House. She shook her head and maneuvered into six inches of unoccupied space on the car. Today, she would enjoy. Tomorrow, she'd get back to her problems.

Commuters and tourists crowded the seats and aisles of the car, allowing little space between bodies. Cari stood in the aisle, gripping a handhold, with Rand inches away. The car tilted going uphill, sending Cari close to Rand, and tilted again going down, sending Rand closer to her.

They disembarked amid a large crowd and Rand paused, waiting for the crowd to thin. ''Ghirardelli

Square and the Cannery to the west, Fisherman's Wharf to the east,'' Rand announced cheerfully. ''They're all within walking distance.''

''Ghirardelli Square is where that big red building owned by a chocolate manufacturer is, isn't it?''

''Domingo Ghirardelli, if I remember the first name correctly, built it. But someone else bought it years ago and restored the building. Today, numerous shops and restaurants fill the area. Great for shopping, I hear.''

''But you're not into shopping today.''

''Sightseeing while you shop.''

''I think my budget could afford some chocolates.''

''On the way back from the wharf might be good.''

''Right. I'd probably eat them before we got out of the shop.'' Cari restrained a giggle. Acting like a teenager on a first date wasn't terribly cool for a professional well over twenty-one. She pulled a sober look across her face as she turned in step with Rand and walked to the wharf. They strolled along the open-air markets, and the sober look fled when they stopped to peer at the red-clawed crabs. Cari wrinkled her nose at the smell, and Rand laughed. She looked up, and his merry eyes met hers. Being sober after that was a lost cause.

They strolled toward the water and watched the ships in the harbor. Fishing boats chugged across the sulky, steel gray water, leaving a dingy ruffle of water in their wake. Even the sky was pewter colored. But Cari scarcely noticed. The sunlight in her heart colored the vista.

Rand chose a restaurant overlooking the bay. The view was as spectacular as any advertisement Cari had dreamed over. The linen was as white as fresh snow, the tableware was shining silver, and the wine in crystal glasses shimmered under the glow of a hurricane candle arrangement.

Cari knew the food must be tasty. But, like the magnificent view, it was only background music to the wonder of meeting Rand's gaze between wisps of commonplace conversation. The time seemed too short when Rand glanced at his watch and looked at her with a sigh.

"We should start back to Buena Vista. You probably have to work tomorrow. I know I do."

Before they reached the cable car stop, Rand turned toward Ghirardelli Square. "We mustn't forget the chocolates."

Cari laughed lightly. "It would be better if we did."

But Rand insisted on entering the candy shop and buying chocolates, which he presented to her with a flourish.

"I thought your budget was tighter than mine," Cari teased. Then she winced when she remembered why his budget was limited. She refused to let the memory linger. Today had been too wonderful to spoil with thoughts of conflict. Tomorrow would be soon enough.

"So I'll eat peanut butter sandwiches for the next week." Rand's humorous voice settled any further thought of Hawthorne House.

"I'll share my chocolates for dessert." Warmth bubbled inside Cari, erupting in a cheerful smile. Again, she felt young and gay when Rand took her hand and they ran for a distant cable car.

On the drive back to Buena Vista, she let the memories surface again. What was she doing, looking at Rand as though he was the answer to every woman's dream? Just because he was handsome and kind and honest and caring . . .

She forced her thoughts to stop spouting praises. He was the man bent on destroying her home. Even if that wasn't a problem, which it was, she knew that long-term relationships only led to heartbreak.

The light was out in the hall leading to their apartments, and Rand took her hand. She knew the way by heart, but she didn't pull away. It felt good. At her door, she paused and said good night and told him she'd had a wonderful day. She was scarcely aware of his reply, for a moment later his mouth found hers.

Chapter Eight

Slinging a towel over his shoulder, Rand headed for
the shower after saying good night to Cari. He let the
tepid water stream over his body, dipping his head
under the spray as if to cool his thoughts. When he
worried about depleting the supply of hot water, he
turned the faucet off, stepped from the stall, dried
slowly, and went back to his room. He picked up a
medical journal he'd borrowed from Jim's library and
began an article that had looked interesting earlier.
This evening, he couldn't focus his attention beyond
the second paragraph. He strolled to the door leading
to the balcony and decided against going out into the
night air. The last time he'd opened the door it had
emitted a squeak like a car alarm sounding off. He'd
meant to see about oiling the hinges, but he'd forgotten. He sighed, wondering if his lovely neighbor was
sleeping. Or could she still be awake? Could she be
thinking of him? Finally he went to bed. But not to
sleep.

His attraction to Cari was getting out of hand. He
hadn't meant to kiss her in the kitchen while he was
rinsing the dishes after the barbecue.

Certainly taking her to Fisherman's Wharf hadn't

been advisable. She already spent too much time in his thoughts, and the heartbreak would be his. For how could she forgive him for destroying her house? He rolled over restlessly and thumped his pillow. He saw no way to avoid buying Hawthorne House if he honored his commitment to the clinic with Jim Barstow. Or his commitment to his father, who'd sold his land to lend him money. He thumped the pillow again. Allowing his heart to rule his head was unthinkable!

For the second morning in a row, Cari bounced out of bed smiling. The afternoon spent with Rand in San Francisco had been wonderful, the drive home pleasant, the kiss on the second-floor landing indescribable.

If only she could forget the unsuccessful marriages of her mother—if only Rand didn't want to tear down her house. Cari grinned wryly and plugged in the coffee maker. *Yeah, right. If only pigs could play the piano. . . .*

She added water and coffee to the coffee maker and went to take a shower. The first spray of cold water banished the remainder of the rosy glow in her head. The water heater again. Shivering, she stepped away from the spray and wet her hands for a skimpy scrub. She hadn't wanted a long shower anyway.

Back in the kitchen, she raised a shade and found the morning as bright as her mood had been on arising. She slid a piece of whole wheat bread into the toaster. At least the electricity still worked. Better a cold shower than no coffee and toast.

It was after three when she saw Rand. She was on call for the evening and night, and she'd hoped there were no cases scheduled after three. She helped transfer her last case to the recovery room and stopped by the nurses' station.

Reba sat at the desk writing on a chart.

''Possible tendon repair in the ER,'' Reba said.

Cari leaned one hip against the desk and made a face. ''How can I say I really want to go home when I know I need the extra money?''

Reba looked up from the paperwork and sighed dramatically. ''What went out this time?''

''Hopefully, only the pilot light on the water heater. I stopped by the Bransons' apartment to tell John, but I didn't wait to see what was wrong.''

''Think positive. A lighted match may solve the problem.''

Cari shrugged. ''With my luck lately, the tank probably rusted through and snuffed out the pilot light and I'll have to replace carpets all over the lower floor—if not warped wooden flooring.''

''Then you can look on the tendon repair as good luck. For you, that is. Not for the poor victim.''

''Good luck?''

''Money to replace a water heater tank, at least.''

Cari laughed. ''That's why you're a good friend. Always cheering me up.''

''Who's the surgeon?''

''Dr. Carson is on call for the orthos.''

Cari couldn't help feeling a flow of warmth.

It was well after four when an emergency room nurse accompanying the injured child handed Cari a chart.

''The young girl,''—the nurse nodded at her patient—''Mindy, and her friend were Rollerblading on the patio. Mindy tried to stop at the French doors leading inside and missed the door frame. She shoved a hand through the glass pane instead.''

The nurse motioned at the bandaged left arm. ''I soaked the hand and arm in diluted betadine. Anesthesia has been notified as well as the OR supervisor.'' She signed off the chart. ''Dr. Carson saw Mindy in the ER. Said you'd know to set up a plastics tray with fine mosquitoes and fine metzenbaums.''

Cari nodded. ''The surgical tech is setting up the instrument tray now.''

Cari pushed the gurney to the operating room and waited for the anesthesiologist to help her move the small patient.

She glanced at the scrub room and felt a blossom of warmth in her chest at the sight of Rand at the scrub sink.

Turning back to help the anesthesiologist, she closed her thoughts to Rand and concentrated on her duties. When the child slept quietly under the skilled ministrations of the anesthetist, Cari applied a tourniquet above the elbow without tightening it. Only then did she remove the blood-stained Kerlix bandages from the arm. A deep two-inch laceration gaped near the wrist, and a number of smaller cuts marred the young girl's fine skin.

She was all business when she fastened Dr. Carson's gown and asked him what kind of suture he would need.

His voice was equally professional as he replied, ''Four-0 nylon for the smaller lacerations. For the other, I'll have to wait until I get in and find out the extent of the damage.''

Cari nodded, stepping back to the side of the table

to prep the injured arm. She lifted the small right hand with her left hand, working her fingers to grasp the child's thumb and suspend the arm in midair. Gently, but thoroughly, Cari scrubbed the skin, working her way up the hand and arm.

When blood oozed from the wound, she looked at Rand. He turned to the anesthetist, directing him to tighten the tourniquet.

Cari glanced at the pressure device. With an average arm, pressure was regulated to the child's blood pressure.

As the tourniquet inflated, the blood flow ebbed and she breathed a sigh of relief and continued her task.

When she'd finished the prep, Rand stepped forward to join her. His gloved hands brushed hers as he took hold of the thumb. This time, it was Cari who helped as Rand grasped the child's hand with sterile stockinette, working the cloth up the arm. With the operating area sterile, he stepped back for the tech to place the remaining sterile covers over the patient.

When she was finished, he stepped to the operating site again and looked at the anesthesiologist. Getting a nod, he accepted scissors from the tech and made his first incision in the stockinette above the injured area. Holding a hand out for an instrument, he slid the small steel forceps inside the cut and probed the area inside.

"Glass." His voice was grim. "As I suspected." He raised his head to look at Cari. "We'll need an X ray."

Minutes later, with the glass fragments located on film, he removed the dangerous shards. Cari breathed a sigh of relief. The surgery was going well. Rand had only to repair the severed tendon.

What seemed like an hour later, Rand was still searching for the retracted tendon.

Cari looked at Rand. Perspiration misted his forehead as he concentrated on the opening in the child's wrist. Cari stepped forward silently, touching the surgeon's brow with a soft cloth. He continued working as if he had felt nothing, and Cari stepped away.

The tenseness in the room was palpable.

Only the beep of the machine monitoring the vital signs of the patient sounded in the room. Seconds stretched into minutes. Cari glanced at the scrub tech, who met her look, her eyes showing her concern for the surgeon and the nerve-wracking task in which he was engaged. Then Rand breathed heavily, and Cari, too, took a breath.

He'd located the tendon.

Tension waned. The anesthesiologist told a joke. The scrub tech's instruments clattered. The monitor beeped, and Rand laughed belatedly.

Putting a last suture in the skin of the small wrist, Rand removed his gloves and applied bandages and a plaster cast and stepped back.

Cari was aware of him watching her while she prepped the child's right leg, but he didn't speak until she stepped away. Then he only murmured ''good job.''

He sutured two small lacerations below the knee with no less diligence than he had displayed with the more serious wound. When he'd completed the last suture, Cari expected him to step back and shed his gloves and gown in relief. But he didn't. He stayed to help bandage the leg he'd sutured.

"Her mother will be pleased to hear she should still be able to play the piano." Rand accepted another bandage from the surgical tech. "Though she may miss playing in a school concert next month." He tried to lighten his voice, but the strain was still evident. "She's quite talented, her mother says."

Cari glanced at him, admiration blurring her vision for a second. Not only had he been under the gun to repair the tendon, he'd carried the extra burden of knowing what it meant to the child's future if he didn't succeed.

She knew it was part of the job, worrying about saving a life or repairing an injury that could impair a child for life. But she couldn't help thinking Rand was special. The strain still showed in his eyes, in the look on his face.

She took a steadying breath, aware her fingers itched to touch Rand's cheek, to smooth away the weariness threatening to carve unwanted lines around his sensual lips. But she went around him and untied his gown and walked to toss it into a hamper. Without speaking, she turned, glad she was needed to assist the anesthetist. Rand had left the room by the time she looked up again.

Cari had little time to reflect on the successful prognosis of the tendon surgery. Answering the telephone had her mind racing to prepare for an accident case and a possible C-section.

Cari glanced at the oversize wall clock as she left a cleaned and reset operating room to walk wearily to the nursing desk. Rand lounged in a chair, a coffee cup in his hand.

He grinned. ''The recovery room nurse said you were almost ready to leave. Thought I should stay and follow you home in case your car is acting up again.''

Gratitude welled in Cari's chest. ''You didn't need to do that. You've had a long day.''

''No longer than yours,'' he said lightly.

But more stressful, Cari thought. The admiration and compassion she'd felt this morning following the tendon surgery threatened to erupt anew. Giving herself a few seconds to steady her emotions, Cari glanced toward the recovery room, letting reality return with the faint sound from a monitor breaking the silence.

''It's not like I lived ten miles away.'' She managed a laugh. ''I could jog if I had to.''

Rand made a face. ''Not a good idea this late, even in quiet little ol' Buena Vista.''

Cari nodded, looking at the coffee carafe longingly. But she'd had enough coffee for the evening. She needed solid food.

''Mind if we stop by the dining room? Maybe I can get a sandwich or something.''

Rand stood and carried his cup to the counter. ''Sure thing.''

In the dining room, Cari slipped change into the food machines and waited with weary impatience for a ham sandwich and a carton of milk. Despite her weariness, she grinned when Rand eyed the sandwich skeptically and slid his coins in to select a carton of chocolate milk.

"Don't scoff," she said. "This has to be tastier than the leftovers in my fridge."

"Or mine." Rand walked to a nearby table. "This okay?"

"Any place I can sit down is okay."

Unwrapping a straw, Cari punched it into the opening of the carton and sighed heavily. "Another day, another dollar to repair the water heater."

"Was that the trouble with the hot water?"

Cari shrugged. "I hope it was only the pilot light."

Rand lifted his eyes toward the ceiling with a wry grin. "Cari, the place is falling apart. Mr. Branson says it's always in need of repairs, and Maggie worries about you. She says you scarcely have a social life. There's no time between work at the hospital and work at the house. Don't you think you'd be better off in a modern, comfortable apartment?"

"Better off, maybe, but not happier. The landlord can't tell me I'm not allowed to have pets in the house or parties past eight. He can't tell me I'm using too much water and electricity isn't free. Or scowl at me if I make a little noise coming down the stairs. Or evict me if I'm late with the rent." Her eyes sobered. The lilt left her voice. "I'll bet you've never had to worry about whether you'd still be living at the same place when you came in from school, or where you'd sleep at night."

Rand's look was compassionate. "No, I haven't, Cari. Even overseas, I knew I belonged somewhere. It might have had a leaky roof and walls that wouldn't keep winds or rats out, but it was home."

"Well, Hawthorne House has a leaky roof and rebellious showers and migrant electricity. But it's my home. I mean to keep it that way.'' She took a gulp of milk and then concentrated on unwrapping the sandwich. ''You could find another location.''

He looked at her soberly. ''The same could apply to you. With the money you receive from the sale, you could make a decent down payment on a new house. No more leaky roofs or obstinate showers or electrical problems.''

''A new house is not one my grandmother gave me.'' How could she tell him her feeling of belonging when she walked through the door and into Hawthorne House? Her grandmother had given her that with the gift of the old house. She liked to imagine she'd grown up in the house—helped her mother cook Thanksgiving dinners, helped a father, any father, decorate a Christmas tree in the living room.

Rand looked glum. ''Cari, I don't want to hurt you. I'd back out of this deal if I could. But I can't.'' He stared at the milk carton before him. ''I'm obligated to so many people.''

''They could find another location,'' Cari said stubbornly.

''Someone else would be banging at your door to sell. The other property owners are going to sell. It's only a matter of time with Mr. McGrath.''

She pushed the sandwich aside. It tasted as stale as her thoughts.

The walk to her car was silent. What else could she say? Rand meant to continue with his project; she meant to stop him.

He was thoughtful, and she was attracted to him more than she ever thought she could be. But there was no future together for her and Rand.

They climbed the stairs side by side, so close Cari's skirt brushed Rand's trousers. But Cari was careful her hand did not touch his.

They stopped at the first landing. Moonlight filtered through the stained-glass window, giving the colors a soft glow. Rand stopped and turned to Cari.

''You were a big help in the operating room today. Just knowing you were there cheering for me helped. Finding that tendon was murderous.''

''But you found it and spliced it back together.'' Cari made her voice light. ''Maybe the little girl will invite you to her first concert.''

''That's the important thing.'' Rand's gaze held Cari's. ''She'll be able to play again.''

Cari pulled her gaze away. He was so good and caring and compassionate. She wanted to touch him and tell him he was wonderful and she was wild about him. She wanted him to hold her and let the moonlit glow through the colored glass cover them with magic. But she knew she wouldn't.

That was another fantasy, like imagining cooking dinner in the big kitchen downstairs and waiting impatiently for Rand to come home from the office. Or trying to decide which apartment upstairs would make the best nursery.

Daydreaming would not change her mind about the house. Nor his. When Rand accepted her decision not to sell, he'd move on to another location. Maybe another city. She had to accept that. Even if the thought was as painful as a laceration.

Rand turned and started up the stairs, and Cari hesitated, falling one step behind. In the hallway, he turned toward his door and she toward hers. His "good night" was muffled. Hers was almost inaudible. Then they entered separate doorways.

Chapter Nine

"Coffee?" Reba asked. She'd already poured a cup and plopped herself in a chair.

"Not today." Cari reached in her locker for a T-shirt. "It's Wednesday."

"And yesterday was Tuesday and you took off early to see the president of the Historical Society."

"Lot of good it did," Cari said dismally. She tucked the colorful shirt into the waistband of a blue gray skort.

"Didn't go too well, huh?"

"I learned it can take up to two years just to get Hawthorne House on the list to be considered." Cari lifted her hands and shook them in frustration. "I don't have two years." Her voice trembled. "I don't have two months if my cousin's husband has anything to say about it."

"Has he called again?"

"Not called. He was waiting on the front porch when I got home from the meeting. As if I didn't feel lower than a basset hound's belly, he lays on a guilt trip about how much my aunt needs money. Not to mention threats. If I don't agree to sell, he will see if Hawthorne House conforms to the city building code or something." Cari sighed heavily.

''Yesterday was not a good day for you, I gather.''

''Even what I did find out didn't help.''

''Like?''

''The Planning Commission has something called an interim control ordinance. A moratorium. It puts a freeze on building permits in a certain area to allow for more planned development. Say too many shops for one type of business. That sort of thing.'' Cari tilted her head dejectedly. ''But there aren't too many medical clinics. Buena Vista could use this one. I just want it to be built on the other side of the hospital.''

''You do need a cup of coffee and a shoulder to lean on.'' Reba set her cup down and stood. ''Sit down right here and I'll wait on you.''

Cari had a fleeting thought of another person who'd waited on her one late evening after work.

''I can't, Reba. I really can't. The City Council meets on Wednesday. I have to pick up my car from the repair shop, and I want to get home and call Ben and see if he plans to attend the meeting this evening.''

''Is he able to?'' Reba poured liquid into a cup, releasing a pungent aroma of coffee in the air.

''Probably not. But if he doesn't, he'll sit at his daughter's house and stew. That could be even worse for his heart.'' Cari took a sip from the cup Reba pushed into her hand. ''I thought I'd offer to go after him and drive him home.''

She set the near full cup down. ''I'll see you to-morrow.''

''Call me when you get in.''

''It might be late.''

''Call me anyway. If you can. You have me worrying about that darned house now.''

* * *

Cari smiled at the sight of Ben's old Cadillac parked in front of his house. Parking her newly repaired car, she pushed open the gate. Her smile broadened. If Ben's daughter had let him drive home to see his roses, he must be improving.

Plus, Cari reasoned, he was probably coming to assure her he would be at the council meeting.

She didn't see him. She walked past the front yard, standing across from the gazebo and scanning the rose garden.

"Ben," she called cheerfully. "Come out, come out, wherever you are."

Only the muted sound of traffic on the next block and the fragrance of rose blossoms filled the air. Then a siren's scream shattered the peacefulness. Cari didn't look toward the street. Living near the hospital, the startling sound had become commonplace. She was more concerned about her elderly friend's whereabouts.

She turned back toward the front of the house. Maybe Ben was inside.

Her eyes scanning the front porch, Cari felt her shoe touch something. She looked down. A pair of rose clippers, with green vinyl covering the handles, lay near her right foot. Leaning over, she picked them up. The clippers were shiny and well cared for. They hadn't been left out overnight. Ben must have been using them.

"Ben!" Cari's voice was hesitant, then she walked purposefully toward the porch.

She didn't reach it.

A patch of color stained the wood chips surrounding

a distant bush. Cari glanced at it. Half a dozen brilliant pink rose petals scattered across the darker background. Which wasn't unusual. Bursting blossoms shed their petals in a gust of wind. Cari almost moved on.

But just beyond the salmon-hued droplets protruded a small mass of yellow no larger than a big toe. Her breath caught in her lungs.

It was a toe, attached to a foot. A foot in a yellow sock. A house shoe lay a few feet away.

''Ben!'' Cari's cry of anguish cut across the roses. She hurried forward and dropped to her knees, unaware of the wood chips pressing into her bare skin. Her sleeve caught on the thorn of a bush and she jerked it free, feeling no pain as the thorn ripped a miniature channel in her arm. With suppressed panic, she reached to check Ben's pulse.

She laid her fingers along Ben's neck, feeling for a pulse in the carotid artery. A faint throb touched the sensitive pads of her fingers. She focused her attention on her right hand. The irregular pressure against her fingers was weak, but it was there. She pulled back, her gaze lowering to his chest. There, too, the movement was weak, but it was visible.

Ben's chest rose, and Cari released her own imprisoned breath. ''Ben.''

He didn't respond.

Scrambling to her feet, Cari raced through the rose garden, yanking at the cotton material of the skort when unyielding thorns threatened to capture her. Dagger points pierced her skin, but she scarcely felt them. She raced on, daring the thorns to delay her.

Leaving the front door open, she hurtled past the staircase and into Maggie's living room.

She almost sagged with relief at the sight of her friend. "Maggie, call the paramedics. I think Ben's had another heart attack. He's in the rose garden." She motioned to an afghan folded on the sofa and didn't wait for a nod from Maggie before she took it. Turning, she sped through the open door.

Let him be alive, she prayed, while all the time trying to remember the rhythm for CPR.

Ben's eyelids quivered as she sank on the ground beside him. Carefully, she spread the crocheted cover over him. Then she lifted her head, listening for the sound of a siren.

When the strident peel rent the air, she thought she'd never heard such a wonderful sound. The paramedics would bring intravenous fluids and medicine to strengthen Ben's heart. The emergency room was only minutes away, but the thought that the ambulance had a defibrillator and respirator aboard was comforting.

The ambulance personnel recognized her before she recognized them. She felt unfocused—except on Ben.

A young, dark-eyed man readied an intravenous fluid setup while Cari told another paramedic of Ben's recent admission to the intensive care unit. The second paramedic relayed the message to a physician in the emergency room.

For a moment, Cari felt helpless as the other medical personnel cared for Ben. When they loaded him onto the stretcher, the communications man looked at Cari.

"Do you want to go to the hospital with him?"

Cari nodded.

Inside the ambulance one of the technicians handed Cari a gauze dressing with disinfectant on it.

Cari looked at him quizzically.

''Your arm,'' the young man said.

Cari looked down and mechanically scrubbed at the blood on her arm while her gaze remained on the paramedic attending to Ben.

It was after ten when she left Margaret and went to the OR. Ben's vital signs were stable and he'd been admitted to the ICU again. Margaret's husband had arrived to stay with her. Cari knew she should go home. Tomorrow was another working day. She pushed the panel to open the doors, half hoping Reba was working. She could walk home, of course. Or jog. Wasn't that what she'd told Rand?

She shook her head. Funny how her thoughts always managed to return to Rand.

She almost turned around to go to a hospital exit. A walk might clear her head. But then she thought of the deserted streets after one left the hospital area. The street to Hawthorne House was even more deserted, and darker. Being in an older district meant streetlights were few and far between—like a corner streetlight with the power of a birthday candle on each block.

She continued on toward the surgical suite. Anyone who was on duty would give her a ride home. She was just reluctant to explain her bloodstained skort and lack of transportation. Which was ridiculous. She was a nurse, after all.

The operating room suite was dimly lit and almost soundless. With a shrug, Cari turned to leave, and the door from the doctors' lounge opened. Rand walked into the room. His head was lowered, his gaze locked on his watch as he fastened the strap, and he looked tired.

"Hi."

He looked up, and the weariness receded with the emergence of a warm smile. "I thought everyone had left."

Cari tilted her head. "They must have. I don't hear anyone in the back." She took a careful breath. She hadn't wanted to see Rand of all people. His hair was neatly combed, and he smelled of soap and lotion. He was dressed in the usual cotton trousers and a light sports coat. Only the unbuttoned collar of a tan-colored shirt gave him a more casual, after-office-hours look. Cari attempted to straighten her disheveled shirt and equally disheveled skort. "Late rounds?"

He nodded. "I came back to get my watch. Went upstairs to see about another patient and remembered I'd left the watch in my locker." He checked the fastening on the watch strap. "What are you doing here so late?"

Cari pursed her lips briefly. "Ben had another heart attack."

Compassion clouded Ran's eyes. "I'm sorry to hear that. How is he?"

Cari took the deep breath she hadn't allowed herself to take earlier. "His vitals are stable. Lab tests are in progress. And he's sleeping, so I thought I'd go home and do the same."

Rand nodded. "I'm glad to see you're taking your own advice."

Cari blinked. "What?"

''The advice.'' Rand chuckled. ''I think you told me that's what you tell relatives who are exhausted.''

''Did I?''

Rand nodded solemnly. ''Isn't that what you told Ben's daughter at the time of his last heart attack?''

''Did I?'' Cari flushed. She was echoing again. Did this happen with anyone but Rand? She cleared her throat nervously. ''Did you have a case this evening?''

''Sure did. And Jim was called out of town to consult on an accident case.'' He made a wry face. ''So neither of us could attend the council meeting. How did it go?''

The council meeting!

Speechless, Cari stared at Rand. The council meeting. She'd forgotten the all-important meeting in the aftermath of finding Ben.

''You did go, didn't you?''

Cari felt as though the sigh she emitted came from the soles of her scuffed tennies. Slowly, she shook her head. ''I guess I forgot after I found Ben.''

''You found him?'' Rand's voice dropped an octave.

Cari nodded. ''His old car was parked in front of the house when I got home from work. I went into the yard to say hello. Ben had fallen among his rosebushes.'' She took a quavery breath. ''I came to the hospital in the ambulance with him, and I just forgot about the meeting.''

Rand reached out and touched her hand. ''There'll be other meetings.''

''Maybe. Maybe not,'' Cari said morosely. ''Depends on what went on in the meeting tonight.''

''Well, Jim and I didn't make it.''

"That lawyer for the other residents probably did."

"The council won't make a decision tonight, so cheer up until you hear bad news."

"Whose side are you on?" Cari said dryly.

Rand grimaced. "Changing the subject, I'll wager you haven't had anything to eat since lunch."

"Lunch? Come to think of it, I worked through lunch so I could get off on time—to attend the council meeting."

He shook his head. "What you need is a little food. Or a lot of food. Like carbohydrates and chocolaty desserts."

"What's this concern you have with my feeding habits?" The wry tone in Cari's voice caught in her throat when she saw the way Rand was looking at her. It wasn't the look of a doctor concerned about the nutrition of a patient.

"I care about you."

Rand's words seemed to echo in the silence of the operating suite. Cari's heart picked up a beat and sent it pulsing to her ears. She smelled the scent of his soap and aftershave, and her fingers tingled with the need to touch his cheek. She wanted to lean against his chest and let him put his arms around her and soothe away the shadows of today: Ben's illness, the missed meeting, the failure with the Historical Society, her cousin's threatening husband.

Rand looked away first, one hand slipping to the stethoscope dangling from his coat pocket as if anchoring himself to reality. When he looked back again, he'd managed to put a sparkle in his eyes. "The body doesn't function too well without filling up the tank regularly, and you're scheduled to work my case tomorrow."

Disappointment that the moment had passed was tinged with relief. Only disaster lay in allowing herself to believe love would find a way to overcome their problem.

Cari turned toward the exit. ''That's why I'm on my way home. I want to be bright and eager tomorrow.''

Rand lifted his eyebrows in feigned delight. ''You can't wait to work with me?'' he teased.

Somehow the success in bypassing the emotional moment made Cari feel gay and reckless. She grinned mischievously. ''I can't afford to miss a paycheck.''

Rand pressed a hand over his heart, his look light and teasing. ''I'm wounded.''

Cari giggled and realized she was tired, physically and emotionally. She needed to get home before she reacted unwisely to Rand's caring banter. ''I don't see any blood, but I can give you directions to the emergency room.''

''I'll recover on my own, thank you. Meanwhile, considering you missed lunch and dinner, we should stop by the dining room and warm a cold sandwich in the microwave. Just to be sure you have energy to work tomorrow.'' He touched her elbow and guided her toward the exit. ''Or we could find a restaurant with something on the menu besides hamburgers or pizza.''

''Spaghetti,'' Cari crooned. ''Do you think we could find a spaghetti house still serving?''

''If we can't find one, I know how to open a can.''

''I'm impressed.'' She dipped her head. ''Mother always wanted me to date a man who could cook.''

''This is a date, then.''

''No. I just said that's what mother wanted. It's a Dutch treat.'' It was a second before she realized she didn't have her purse. She must have dropped it on Ben's lawn. She shoved her hands into the pockets of her skort and grimaced. She didn't have so much as an emergency coin to call a cab, let alone money to pay for dinner. She pulled her hands from her pockets and ran them along the sides of the stained skort. ''Considering I look a little tattered and torn, maybe the can of spaghetti is the best idea.''

Chapter Ten

"A stroke?" Cari stared at the intensive care nurse. "When?"

The nurse opened a chart, checking the notations. The tall, slender, thirtyish nurse wore white pants and a pale blue tunic with bulging pockets. But her hair, upswept on the sides and fashioned into a roll in the back, looked as pristine as if she'd just left the beauty salon. Cari unconsciously pushed an errant lock from her own forehead.

"Three-fifteen this morning." The nurse continued to study the notes.

Cari glanced away, noting the activity in a glass-enclosed room across from the central desk. An elderly woman had managed to slide to the end of the bed, bypassing the protective side rails. She thrust one frail foot from beneath the sheet and tried to evade the nurse beside her. The nurse before Cari lifted her gaze from the chart, glanced at the commotion, and grimaced gently. "She doesn't want to use our bedpans."

"Who does?" Cari grinned automatically. She turned back to face the informative nurse. "Have you called Ben's daughter?"

The nurse shook her head. "The doctor plans to call

her later this morning. She was here until two. He said she needs a little rest.''

Cari tilted her head and lifted her eyebrows in response. ''Is Ben conscious?''

The nurse closed the chart and returned it to a circular rack. ''In and out.''

''Can I see him? I'll just stay a minute. I'm circulating on a case at seven this morning.''

''Sure.'' The nurse glanced at the monitor and back at Cari. ''I'll call the OR and leave a message if there is a significant change in his condition.''

''Thanks.'' Cari hitched up the sleeves of her cover gown. She'd changed into scrubs and checked in with her supervisor before running up the back stairs to say hello to her friend. Now, she made her way across the circular-shaped department to the glass-enclosed room where Ben lay immobile on his narrow bed. Intravenous tubes and monitor lines connected his body to monitors and fluid bags. Cari felt a sense of despair. Ben looked frail and helpless and not at all like the cheerful, teasing Ben she'd come to love. She touched his hand and called his name, waiting anxiously for a response. He didn't flicker an eyelash.

Heavyhearted, she left the ICU and made her way to the OR.

By the time she went back to see Ben that afternoon, he was responsive. Cari's heart lightened. He wasn't jumping out of bed at her arrival, but he did recognize her. Maybe the stroke wasn't as bad as she feared.

The following days, she visited every afternoon, watching his slow improvement until he was transferred to the medical floor and then to the rehabilitation unit. She always seemed to be rushing to do something when she saw Rand at work, and their off time didn't coincide. She thought about the council meeting briefly but forgot to try to find out the results. It was over a week later when she paused long enough to have coffee with Reba after work.

Reba scowled at her in mock displeasure. ''When are you going to slow down?'' Reba scolded. ''Your eyes are glazed, and you're beginning to look like a bag lady who can't find a place to sleep.''

Cari made a face and trudged to the coffee counter. ''I am a little tired.'' She filled a cup and crumpled into a nearby chair.

''You can't keep staying with Ben half the night and working extra call time too.''

''You would have stayed too if you'd seen Ben's eyes. He was so frightened when he had difficulty talking and moving his right hand. Having someone familiar around seemed to calm him when he was transferred to the medical floor. His daughter couldn't stay all the time. She has two children and her husband is away a lot.''

''You have a fuller-than-full-time job.''

''I know. But Ben was so bewildered at the transfer to the rehab center.''

''How is he now?''

''Better. He's been able to speak for the last two days with only a little slurring in his words. His daughter feels more comfortable staying with him now, so I'm not going to stay this evening. I've got to do some laundry and wash a few dishes. And check on Ben's roses.''

"Check on Ben's roses?"

"I promised I'd keep an eye on them."

"I suppose you plan to water, weed, and fertilize after midnight."

"No. I expect Margaret and her husband will do that."

"So you have the coming weekend off?"

"Half of it. I promised to take call Saturday."

"I can work around that."

Cari lifted an eyebrow quizzically.

"Sissy's birthday."

Cari popped her forehead with an open palm. "Sissy's birthday! How could I have forgotten?"

"You have been a little busy."

"Dinner Friday night, right?"

"Right. Saturday afternoon, Mom is having a kids' party, which you're invited to also—if you can get off work. Friday's dinner is for the family."

"It's nice to be included with the family."

"We wouldn't have it any other way. Bring a change of clothes tomorrow, and we'll leave from work. I need to get there early to help Mom with dinner. Oh, and plan to spend the night."

"I'm on call Saturday, remember."

"You can still spend the night. You just need to get up a little earlier to get back to your place by seven. Come on. You need to get away for a day."

"Are we taking two cars?"

"I can ride with you."

"You're coming back with me at seven in the morning?"

Reba giggled. "I'm coming back with Greg Saturday night."

''Oh.'' Cari rolled her eyes. ''When is Greg driving to your folks?''

''Friday evening.''

''Ah, part of the family. This must be getting serious.''

''I'd like to think so.'' This time Reba rolled her eyes and grinned broadly.

Leaving, Cari didn't even scan the halls or look across the street at the medical offices as she made her way to the hospital parking lot. Even if Rand had popped up right in front of her, she would have been too tired to talk. She grinned involuntarily. Well, not that tired.

Parking her car in front of Hawthorne House, she looked at Ben's yard. Two men worked energetically in the rose garden. Cari took a deep breath. She needn't have worried that Margaret wouldn't see that Ben's roses were cared for.

She entered the old-fashioned, stained-glass door and bypassed Maggie's rooms. Even the fragrant aroma of coffee offered little competition at the thought of a shower. Which would have to wait until she did the laundry, she told herself sternly.

But she couldn't help stopping outside her door to look across the hall. Rand would still be seeing patients in the office at this hour. Then he'd make rounds at the hospital. Or maybe operate on a case that had been scheduled after office hours. Or see an accident case in the emergency room.

She sighed. They worked in the same building and lived in the same house, but she'd scarcely seen him all week. She thought about him at the oddest times.

Her heart skipped a beat if she saw him in the operating room, but they did little more than say ''hi'' and
''see ya.''

Which was good, she reminded herself. Getting involved emotionally with Rand would only lead to a
broken heart. Hers.

She collected her soiled clothes and went downstairs to the washing machine on the service porch.
She turned the dial to ''Extra-large load,'' started the
water, and added clothes and detergent. She thought
about Maggie's coffee and forced herself to go back
to her apartment. The dishes wouldn't wash themselves.

With the dishes drying in a drainer, she went downstairs again to shift the wet clothes to the dryer—
which wouldn't start. She groaned, hoping someone
had only unplugged the machine. She was too tired to
take a ton of damp clothes to the laundromat across
town.

She leaned over the dryer, straining to see the power
outlet. A tangle of electric wires drooped behind the
electrical appliances. But the heavy cord from the
dryer seemed to be plugged into place. She shifted her
weight to the floor again and reset the dial. This time,
a whirring sound filled the air. Cari breathed easier.
She had time for a shower before the clothes were
ready to come out.

Friday afternoon, she and Reba left the hospital
early for the hour's drive to the family farm. Cari
opened the car windows, breathing in the warm spring
air. They chatted about a continuing education class
for operating room nurses scheduled in San Francisco.

Both moaned they couldn't afford the hotel room, let alone the fee for the class. But it sounded good—to have an excuse to get away to San Francisco.

Cari's mind bobbed back and forth between the memories of her evening in the "city by the bay" with Rand and the conversation. Going to San Francisco could never be the same with someone else. She'd picture Rand's hair tousled by the wind and hear his humorous voice. She'd smell the sea mixed with the scent of his aftershave. She'd think of the Golden Gate Bridge and imagine the warmth of his eyes as he gazed at her across the table where they'd dined. She reached down and flicked on the car radio and shifted the topic of conversation.

Saturday morning, she was back in Buena Vista before seven with a new catalog of memories. But she didn't have long to think about them. The telephone rang at seven-twenty.

She worked until five that afternoon, had a snack in the hospital dining room, and went to visit Ben. She felt guilty. She couldn't honestly say she'd checked on the roses in two days. But she could tell him his daughter had someone taking care of them. And short of a swarm of locusts or whatever attacked roses, what could happen to healthy rosebushes in two days?

Nevertheless, she was glad Ben was napping when she saw him. Honesty was one of her failings. She didn't have to tell him she'd just left his yard and the roses were fine when she hadn't looked toward his yard since Thursday.

Her beeper sounded as she crossed the parking lot to return to her car. She moaned and drove to the hospital, all the time reminding herself the Hawthorne House repair fund was growing with every ache of her feet.

Working until eleven, she didn't even glance toward Ben's house when she trudged up her front walk to the familiar stained-glass door.

It was almost noon when she awoke Sunday. She plugged in the coffee maker, added water and coffee, and returned to her bedroom to change. Minutes later, dressed in shorts and a colorful T-shirt, she poured coffee and took her cup out to the balcony to sit in the old rattan chair.

A few minutes later, she heard the door from Rand's room to the balcony open. She wished she'd put on lipstick.

"Hi. Mind if I join you?"

Half a dozen words—like delighted, overjoyed, and it would make my day—bubbled in Cari's head. But she smiled and put her feet up on the old rattan footstool. "Only if you bring your own cup and go in and pour your own coffee. I don't think I can move for the next thirty minutes."

"You had one heck of a long day yesterday. You were still working when I left the hospital at ten."

"You had a case earlier, didn't you? I was busy in another room and had to call the backup crew for your case."

"I know. I missed working with you."

Cari grinned. She'd missed Rand. Working and staying with Ben had taken up most of her waking hours. During the few times she had worked with him, there never seemed to be a moment to say more than a few polite words. "I stopped by to say hello, but you were having an intense moment with a fractured femur.''

''You were struggling to hold a patient who didn't want to have his hand strapped to the IV board when I stopped at the door of your room.''

Cari laughed. ''Life in the OR is interesting. Seldom a dull moment.''

''Makes having a peaceful cup of coffee on Sunday morning a treat.'' He raised one finger. ''I'll get a cup and be right back.'' He turned toward his room.

Cari sat upright. ''Wait. I was teasing about waiting on yourself. I'll get you a cup of coffee.''

Rand held his palm open in a stop sign movement. ''I know where the cups are in your cupboard.'' He strode past Cari before she had her feet on the floor and returned a few minutes later.

Cari wrinkled her face in a comic frown. ''I didn't want you to see my breakfast dishes. I've scarcely been home since I left for work Friday morning.''

Rand placed his cup on the weathered coffee table and repositioned a somewhat newer plastic lounge chair before he sat down. ''You missed the excitement around here.''

''The Saturday night barbecue. I did, didn't I?''

''Plus all the neighborhood news.'' He picked up his coffee cup. But before he could raise it to his lips, the ring of the telephone in his room sounded. He put the cup down and stood up. ''What did I say about a peaceful cup of coffee?''

Cari chuckled and stood up, reaching to pick up her coffee cup and take it to the edge of the balcony. She blinked as she moved from the shade over her chair to the glare of the midday sun. She took a deep, contented breath and gazed at the distant mountains. It was worth working long days to have a home like this. She took a sip of coffee before she turned her gaze toward Ben's yard.

The liquid caught in her throat as she gasped.

The brilliant sun spotlighted each gaping hole where rosebushes once cast a blaze of color over the yard. Cari coughed, clearing her throat as she stared transfixed at the ravaged garden.

Vandals. Thieves. How could someone be so cruel? Her shoulders slumped and the coffee in her cup dripped on the wooden floor. Ben's roses were valuable. Most of them were name-brand bushes with little metal tags identifying then. But their value to Ben was worth more than money. How could she tell him she hadn't protected his treasures? He'd have another heart attack.

She didn't hear Rand return. Tears welled in her eyes and streamed down her cheeks.

''Cari.''

Rand's concerned voice echoed in her ears as she set the coffee cup on the balcony rail and turned and ran inside her room. She didn't stop to close her door before she raced down the stairs. Nor did she close the front door. She didn't stop until she reached Ben's yard.

Sobs shook her slender shoulders as she stumbled from hole to gaping hole. Only a few brilliant petals were left of what was once a magnificent garden. She plunged past the holes and around the side of the house, daring to hope the plunder hadn't proceeded to the backyard. But there too, the rosebushes were missing. The white gazebo stood alone, reigning over gaping holes. Cari closed her eyes, shutting out the damaged yard, and took a long, shuddering breath.

She didn't hear Rand's footstep. She vaguely heard his voice. But she felt the touch of his hand. The feel of his arms as he enfolded her and drew her against his chest. She allowed herself to rest there, letting the strong, steady beat of his heart and the smell of his scent-softened shirt wrap around her.

"How can I ever tell Ben?" Her voice sounded muffled. She pushed away from the strength of his body and raised tear-filled eyes. "I told him I'd take care of his roses. Give him a daily report." She gazed at Rand through a veil of tears. "You knew about it?"

He nodded.

"Of course. That's what you meant by the excitement . . . the neighborhood news at the barbecue."

Rand nodded again.

She ran a forefinger across her cheeks, brushing away the latest tears. "At least the gazebo is intact." Walking to the snowy white structure, Cari climbed the steps dejectedly and sank onto a slatted bench.

She watched Rand follow. He leaned against the open entry and gazed at the plundered garden with distress in his eyes. When he turned to look at her, she saw the distress deepen, and he looked away again. She was touched, knowing he too was upset by the vandalism. She shouldn't be surprised, she told herself. It wasn't out of character. Rand was compassionate and caring. Hadn't she noticed it half a dozen times? The memory of his relief when he'd been able to repair a young girl's tendon so she might resume her musical career. The evenings he'd gone back to check on his cases more than once. His continuing interest in Delia's son's progress, even taking him to practice one afternoon when Delia was at work.

Rand leaned against the post, gazing at the ground. How could he tell Cari the roses had been moved to Ben's daughter's yard and that the gazebo was scheduled to be moved on Monday? How could he tell her this was just a prelude to the sale of Ben's house?

He climbed the final step and sat beside her. ''Ben will see his roses again.''

''You can't be sure.''

''Think positive.'' Rand's voice struggled for humor.

''Optimism rates pretty low with me right now.''

''You're at war with the message on your T-shirt.''

''My T-shirt?'' Cari stared at Rand, who was looking steadfastly at the plundered garden.

He moved his eyes, letting them flit toward the T-shirt before a ragged grin spread across his face. ''Red robins making wedding plans on a snow-encrusted branch.''

Cari giggled weakly. ''Maggie is a romantic.''

''She's just showing that the sun comes out and the snow melts and the robins live happily ever after.''

''It is Maggie's favorite theme, isn't it?''

''It's not a bad one. Especially served with Irish crème or hazelnut coffee and her upbeat attitude.''

Cari straightened the optimistic shirt. ''Be careful. She'll offer you one of her romance novels if she knows she's making a convert.''

''Has she converted you?'' His grin was a little stronger.

''I don't have time to read, and Maggie's heard my opinion of happy endings more than once.''

''Maggie is lucky to have a friend like you. I've seen you stop by to chat when I know you'd rather go upstairs and put your feet up.''

''It's a two-way street. Maggie thinks she's bribing me with fancy coffee to stop by and chat a minute. Actually, I'd walk a mile to have coffee with her. It's not the coffee, it's the 'cookies-and-milk' feeling.''

Rand dipped his head. ''My mother was a milk-and-cookies advocate. In junior high, it was lemonade and taco strips with salsa when I came in from school.''

''Lemonade and salsa?'' The memory of Ben's plundered roses hovered in a yet-to-be-reported police report.

''Today, it's probably root beer and pizza.''

Cari grimaced. ''When I came home from school, I was lucky if we still lived in the same room. Or found anything to eat, since Mom shopped as haphazardly as she cooked.''

Rand's jaw tensed. Delaying telling her Ben's daughter meant to move the gazebo on Monday wouldn't help. She had to know. She had to know that she shouldn't plan for Ben to return home. That Ben's daughter meant to encourage him to sell the house.

Shock, then anger, would well in the lovely eyes that had recently flowed with tears. Then hatred. Part of it would be directed at him.

He could ignore the knowledge. Let her find out Monday that the gazebo was gone and Ben wasn't coming home. But he couldn't let her think robbers had stolen Ben's roses. That would make her even more unhappy than knowing his daughter had had them moved.

He took a breath. ''Ben's daughter had the roses

moved to her yard,'' Rand said before he could change his mind.

''Why?'' Shock spread across Cari's face.

''Ben won't be able to come home for some time. You know he'll need to stay in rehab for a while. He could come home with a nurse and a housekeeper, but with his heart problem and a stroke, Margaret is quite worried.''

''You talked to Margaret?''

''She came to see that the men were taking care with the rosebushes yesterday. She wants to do what's best for her father.''

''Moving him away from his roses isn't the best thing to do for him.''

''She's not moving him away from his roses. She's taking the roses to him.''

''To the rehab center!'' Cari scoffed.

''To her house. She said she'll erect the gazebo where he can walk to it from his room and plant the rosebushes nearby.''

''Has she told Ben?''

''Yes. She said he was rebellious at first. Even when she assured him their gardener could care for his roses until he got out of the hospital. Margaret thinks he relented when she told him the roses would thrive away from the exhaust fumes.''

''But this is Ben's home. He's said a million times he doesn't want to leave it.''

''Home is where Ben's rose garden is, I think.'' Rand's voice was low. ''His house needs even more repairs than yours does.'' He halted abruptly, sorry he'd mentioned Cari's house.

''Which means you think Ben will sell now.''

There it was, the flat, dismal tone he'd dreaded. He couldn't look at her. He couldn't bear to see the despair in her eyes. He couldn't bear to see it change to hatred. At this moment, he'd give anything to be able to tell her to keep the house. To tell her he loved her and that was all that mattered. But he couldn't. He wasn't the only one concerned.

Chapter Eleven

Cari visited Ben Sunday evening, and finding him surrounded by friends and family, she managed to avoid the subject of roses and houses. On Wednesday afternoon, she knew it wouldn't be that easy. Neither Margaret, Ben's grandchildren nor any friends were there. Even the patient who had been in the other bed was gone.

Ben sat in a wheelchair, staring dejectedly out the window of the modest two-bed room.

Cari hesitated for a moment, setting a smile on her face while she prepared to call out in an equally cheerful voice. "Hi! Beautiful afternoon out there. I'll bet you've been waiting for me to push you to the patio."

Ben turned his head slowly. The smile was even slower to arrive. "Hi, Cari. Nice of you to come by."

"You'll think it's even nicer when you see what I've brought." She lifted a bag for him to see. "Chips, dips, nuts, and soft drinks sound good?"

Ben nodded without enthusiasm.

"I went by the patio. We may have it all to ourselves. If not, there's plenty for guests."

"Margaret was here earlier. I don't think she's coming back," Ben grumbled.

''I meant other patients. Course, I'll check with the nurses to see if the goodies are on their diet.''

Ben grinned, but Cari could tell it took an effort. She glanced at his feet. ''I see you have your slippers on, so shall we travel?''

She handed Ben the bag, waiting for him to settle it on his lap before she moved the chair.

The patio was unoccupied when Cari wheeled the chair across the concrete. Several decorative white iron tables with heavy plastic tops were placed well apart, allowing space for wheelchairs to maneuver between them. Matching chairs and benches, shadowed with the lattice design of the roof covering, filled other spaces. A riot of color surrounded the furniture.

Purple-and-yellow pansies peeked from a ground cover of wood chips. A five-foot azalea bush displayed pale pink, palm-sized blossoms. A dwarf palm in a dull red tub spread its wide, fan-shaped leaves protectively over clusters of pink-and-white stock and butter-colored jonquils.

Cari wheeled the chair to a stop at the nearest table. ''Someone even planted that lovely lavender flower that smells so good,'' Cari marveled aloud.

''Hyacinth,'' Ben said grudgingly.

''I'll remember that,'' Cari said cheerfully. She nodded toward a split leaf plant. ''I know what a philodendron is, but what's the plant with the lovely emerald leaves streaked with ruby lines?''

Ben barely glanced at the potted plant. ''That's a maranta. It's a houseplant, usually.''

''Maybe a patient left it.'' Cari put the brakes on the wheelchair and took the bag from Ben. At least he was talking a little.

"It's all so pretty." Cari unloaded the bag, opening bags of chips and salsa and dip. "I remember you liked the onion dip we had at one of our barbecues. I hope this is the right one."

Ben stared at the container glumly. "I guess I won't be going to any more barbecues."

Cari lifted the lid on the onion dip. "Maybe not this Saturday, but in a few weeks I'll be by to get you—wheelchair and all—if you're not jogging."

"I'm not going home, you know," Ben said dully.

"I know." She lifted a soft drink can and slid a fingernail under the circle on top to lift the tab.

"Did you notice the gardenia bush?" Cari scooped ice from a bag into a plastic glass, then filled the glass with the contents of the can. "I like gardenias." She set the glass in front of Ben. "But they can't compare to your gorgeous roses."

"They *were* gorgeous," Ben said gruffly.

"I'm sure they still are. Moving them into the fresh air may be good for them."

Ben snorted. "Some of them are old like me. Moving isn't good for them. Or me."

"Not the best thing, maybe, but sometimes we have to change when circumstances change. Margaret only wants to do what's best for you."

"Did you know she was going to move the bushes?"

"It was a surprise to me." No need to tell him it had been more than a surprise.

"I told her to tell you before she moved them," he said defensively. "I knew you'd be hurt. You'd think I was moving to Margaret's and deserting you."

"Margaret called me Monday and apologized. Said

you'd wanted her to call me and she hadn't been able to reach me earlier.''

"It doesn't mean I'm selling the house," Ben said stubbornly.

"I know. I'm not planning to sell either. So don't worry about it today. I have a few things in mind yet."

Ben's eyes flickered with a tinge of interest. "For instance?"

Cari finished opening packages and cans while she told him about the moratorium.

Ben squinted and tilted his head. "I don't know, Cari. If I recall, that's for things like environmental problems—like not building on land that kangaroo rats inhabit or too much traffic for the area or too many cigar stores on one block. Do you really think we qualify?"

"It's just something to look into. I also thought I could mortgage the house and get enough to buy my aunt's half. They can't force me to sell, can they?"

"I don't think so." Ben chuckled. "I saw a lone house once in a shopping mall."

Cari dragged a chip through the onion dip and tasted it before she spoke again. "Enough of that. Let me tell you about my weekend. Actually, only Friday evening. I went to a birthday party for Reba's sister, Sissy. I know you've heard me mention her." She dipped a chip in the salsa. "Reba's latest boyfriend came. You know,"—she waved the red-tipped chip in the air,— "I wouldn't be surprised if we hear wedding bells in the near future. He can't keep his eyes off her. And she's crazy about him."

Ben's grin erased his former grumpiness. "When am I going to hear wedding bells in your future?"

Cari frowned, but her eyes were laughing. "Trying to palm me off on someone else? Is some younger nurse trying to take my place?"

"Never." Ben said. "But I don't want you to think you have to wait for me to get well. I expect you to go out and have a good time. In fact, I insist on it."

"I haven't had time to meet any men lately."

"How about one you've already met?"

"Aha. You've been talking to Maggie."

"She only told me you went to San Francisco with the doctor who lives at the house. She seems to think he's the ideal man for you."

"That 'ideal man for me' is about to move Maggie's home out from under her, and she sees only a Prince Charming."

"Ah." Ben narrowed his eyes. "The one who wants to build a clinic."

"That's him."

Ben nodded somberly. "That does pose a problem."

"It does indeed," Cari agreed. More than I like to think about.

Preparations for the Saturday barbecue were underway on the patio if the sounds coming through the window were any indication, Cari thought. She stood in the spacious kitchen of Hawthorne House slicing cold, crisp celery to add to the potatoes she'd already diced. Rand stood at the end of the long counter shredding red cabbage with a long chef's knife, turning the purple ball into colorful ribbons stacked on the cutting board.

Scooping the celery atop the potatoes, Cari reached

for a jar of pimentos. It seemed difficult to believe it had been less than a month since Rand had moved into the apartment upstairs. He seemed as at home in the kitchen of Hawthorne House as in the operating room. She knew he stopped to say hello to Maggie after office hours. He played with Joey on weekends. She'd even seen him chatting with John, handing him tools as he repaired a leaky faucet. Her plan to get him involved with his fellow occupants of Hawthorne House hadn't failed. But her efforts to discourage the purchase of Hawthorne House had.

''The cabbage is sliced. What next?'' Rand asked.

''You're sure you want to do this?''

''How hard can it be for a man who's able to follow directions in a surgical text?''

''Okay. Maggie's recipe is on the refrigerator door behind the stuffed pig magnet.'' She added the colorful pimentos to the salad. ''The vinegar is on the shelf next to you. The oil is there also. You know where the sugar, salt, and pepper are.''

Rand made an ''uh-huh'' sound without looking up from the printed recipe, and Cari went back to slicing pickles. She almost purred. The aroma of baked beans simmering in the Crockpot pervaded the kitchen. The ribs were marinating in the refrigerator. And the man of her dreams was poring over a red cabbage salad recipe beside her.

She sighed and came back to reality. If it were only so simple.

''Sorry I was late getting here to help.'' Rand recapped the vinegar bottle.

''It's okay. I knew you were on call. Figured you

were in the ER and hoped I wouldn't get called in too.''

Rand didn't say anything.

''Is the ER busy?'' Cari asked.

''I wasn't in the ER,'' Rand said gruffly.

Cari wrinkled her forehead in puzzlement. Did he think she was prying into what he did with his time off?

''I'm sorry. I wasn't asking where you were.''

Only the bubbling from the Crockpot filled the air for a moment. ''I was at a meeting with Jim and the developer who owns the houses next door to you.''

A chill touched Cari's heart. ''I hope you were canceling your option to buy the houses.''

''No.'' Rand studied the recipe so long, Cari thought he was rewriting it. Finally, he looked up. ''Jim wants to get on with it before they raise the price.''

Cari scowled, her thoughts turning as sour as pickle juice. ''You're not worried about being stuck with the houses when the zoning change doesn't go through?''

''We've talked to enough people to believe we will have no problem there.'' His voice was glum. No evidence of the elation he should be exhibiting. ''It may take a little while.''

''What about Ben's house?''

''Considering Ben's condition, and our talk with his daughter, it's a matter of time until Ben gets used to the idea of not returning to the house.''

Cari reached for another pickled cucumber, her heart feeling as cold as the refrigerated jar that touched her fingers.

''You realize I have no intention of selling.''

''I know. We'll just have to work around that.'' He cleared his throat. ''Maybe downsize the clinic plans.''

''Just so you're prepared.'' She added the final ingredients to the salad.

''Sounds like you've come to an agreement with your aunt.''

''I will. She only wants her money from the sale of the house. I'm going to the bank next week to see if I can borrow enough money on the house to buy her share,'' Cari said, the strength in her voice daring him to doubt the success of her venture.

Rand nodded, his eyes dull, and Cari turned back to the cutting board. For moments, only the clacking of Cari's knife contacting the wooden surface filled the air. Then Rand broke the silence in a voice straining for cheerfulness.

''Where's Maggie?''

Cari plopped another pickle on the board, split it in half with the knife, and took a breath. When she spoke, her voice was calm. ''She's with John. He's having trouble with the lights on the patio, so he's trying to repair the problem before dark.'' Determined to meet Rand's efforts to get along, she grinned and held up a hand in mock warning. ''Don't say it. I know. Another problem.''

From the corner of her eye, she saw Joey's mother walking through the door, her hands filled with a dessert platter. Joey's father followed with bags of rolls and bread. Cari covered the salad bowl with plastic wrap and turned to greet them like long-lost relatives. Keeping up any kind of conversation with Rand was nerve wracking.

Jolene Smith placed a large, plastic-covered plate

on the counter. "We thought we'd stop and see if you needed any help," she chirped cheerfully. "Also, Kent needs to slice the bread." She looked toward her ex-husband with unusual warmth, and Cari lifted an eyebrow. Love must be in the air. First Reba, now Jolene.

She had no time to expand on the thought as Joey entered on the heels of his father. The exuberant preschooler wanted a share of everyone's attention, especially Rand's.

Between questions, Joey helped Rand take the marinated ribs from the refrigerator and carry them to John. He trailed behind Rand when he returned for ice and soft drinks. At some point, he finally deserted Rand to trail behind his father as he carried a stereo set to the patio.

Placing a thoroughly stripped rib on her plate, Cari thought the dinner was unusually good. Through lowered lashes, she gazed at the familiar faces of her friends, as if trying to impress the image of their cheerful faces on a page in her memory. This could be one of the last barbecues they would all be together. From the looks Jolene and Kent exchanged, it seemed they would be looking for a larger apartment to share. Rand would move, of course, when the construction on the clinic started. Cari's heart trembled, and she passed by his face quickly. A smaller clinic, since the plan to purchase the five houses on Oak Street hadn't materialized.

She glanced across the table at Rand. He wouldn't be sleeping across the hall anymore. She wouldn't expect to meet him on the stairs or in Maggie's kitchen. Or at a barbecue. He would be her next-door neighbor, but could he be more than barely civil to her when her refusal to sell damaged his plans?

Lifting a glass of iced tea, she took a swallow and found the liquid slipping past the lump in her throat with difficulty. She looked at her near empty plate, glad she hadn't scooped her usual amount of food on it. Her appetite had waned under the gloom of her thoughts.

After dinner, Kent rose and walked to the stereo equipment he had placed on the patio. He switched on the set, and soft strains of music floated across the air. ''I thought we might have a little dancing after dinner,'' he said jovially. His eyes flicked toward his ex-wife.

Cari lifted her eyebrows. ''Where did you find an extra plug?''

Kent grinned. ''It wasn't easy. But well worth it, don't you think? Listen to that music.'' He looked at his ex-wife and his smile broadened. ''Bring back memories?''

Jolene laughed softly. ''I recognize the melody.''

''That's just for starters. I brought some country tapes—some Reba McIntyres and Alan Jacksons.''

From the corner of her eye, Cari caught a glimpse of John's face. He wasn't smiling. But Rand was standing, walking around the table toward her with a smile on his face. Any concern she might have felt over an extra outlet, added to the earlier electrical problem, fled. Along with the morbid thought of Rand as a next-door neighbor in a new clinic.

She stood, touching the hand Rand extended. One dance, she thought, a first and last. Another memory. Like the memories of San Francisco—thoughts to keep her company on a lonely night. With a smile, she moved into his arms.

The odor of barbecued food faded with the new scent of male aftershave. Rand moved Cari closer, pressing her body lightly against his. Blood pulsed in her throat, and a wave of giddiness touched her. Her lips hovered near his chin. All she had to do was tilt her head. . . . She stopped the thought with a jolt. Dancing was all she'd bargained for. And all she would get, she realized, as her beeper sounded. By the time she'd clicked the sound off, Rand's beeper sounded.

She called in first and made a made a wry face of disappointment. Somehow, she'd hoped the case would be orthopedic. ''C-section.'' She handed the telephone to Rand.

He caught her hand as she turned to leave, holding her while he spoke into the telephone. He didn't release her hand when he hung up. ''Motorcycle accident.''

Cari looked at her hand clasped in his. ''I have to run up and get my purse.''

Slowly, he released her fingers. ''I should get a jacket—look a little professional.''

They walked up the stairs together, near enough to touch, and yet not touching, turned into separate rooms, and met in the hall moments later.

''Can I give you a ride?'' Rand asked.

Cari shook her head. ''Since it's a weekend, I may be in the operating room all night.''

Rand nodded, seemingly as reluctant to leave Cari as she was to leave him. ''Thank you for the dance.''

Cari's fingers clutched the leather of her purse. ''My

pleasure.'' The words felt stiff and formal, and she swallowed, as if she wanted to say more.

''We should go out dancing some evening.''

Cari glanced toward the stairs without moving. ''That would be nice.''

''Only nice?''

With an unusual ache in her heart, Cari lifted her head to look at Rand. ''You don't have to be polite. I know I've hurt your clinic plans with my refusal to sell. I know you think I'm stubborn and unreasonable and . . .''

His head moved up and down in a slow nod, but his eyes never wavered. ''And I love you anyway.''

Cari's breath pooled in her chest. Rand loved her.

Rand's case, a compound fracture, was waiting when Cari helped transport the new mother of twins to the recovery room. The cesarean section had gone smoothly, and the doctor, usually a grouch at any hour, thanked the operating room nurses in a tone akin to civility.

Watching Rand skillfully maneuver the protruding bone beneath the surface of the skin, Cari felt a now familiar ache in her heart. She wouldn't sell her house but he loved her anyway. It was awesome. For a fleeting moment, it made her question the importance she put on owning Hawthorne House.

By the time Cari had helped transport the patient to the recovery room, she was eager to talk to Rand. To . . . She hesitated, confusion whirling in her head. To tell him she loved him? To tell him she'd rethink her position on the house? But he was leaving to visit a post-op patient on the surgical floor. She watched him walk away and turned, walking to the used surgical room to help with the cleaning up.

Driving home, her fingers fidgeted on the steering wheel. She was anxious to get home. Maybe Rand was still up.

She saw the flames as she turned the corner on Oak Street. Glancing quickly in the rearview mirror for an approaching fire engine, she thought of the unoccupied houses next to her home. With a flare of anger, she unconsciously—and unfairly, as it later turned out— attributed the blaze to the shadowy homeless people she'd seen near the hospital. She remembered the young woman, a glowing cigarette wobbling between unsteady fingers, who'd refused an offer to be driven to the city shelter. She'd replied languidly that sleeping under an overpass was preferable, if she couldn't find a vacant house. At the time, Cari hadn't seen any harm in the woman's choosing to sleep in an empty house for a night. She hadn't thought about the danger of a lighted cigarette.

Until now. Until Hawthorne House was threatened.

Nearing the house, she braked for a pajama-clad pedestrian, and her foot froze on the pedal. The back porch of Hawthorne House was in flames.

Behind her, the scream of a siren erupted, and she automatically removed her foot from the brake and pressed the gas pedal to move to the side of the street. She parked the car and loped down the sidewalk, scarcely aware of the people crossing in front of her to stop and stare at the flames.

On the patchy lawn in front of the house, Joey and his mother huddled in their nightclothes. Cari scanned the porch as she bent over Jolene, asking about John and Maggie.

"Maggie said John had gone to the drugstore to get her some ibuprofen. She smelled the smoke after he left and called me, and I carried Joey outside. I thought she was right behind." Jolene's voice broke. "But I guess she tried to go out the back way—where the ramp is. She didn't know that's where the fire started."

Cari stood up and took two steps before Jolene's voice halted her. "Wait. Rand came just before you. He's inside. He went inside to get Maggie."

Cari's heart lurched. Without a thought to the smoke billowing from a window, Cari raced inside.

She sped past the living room, past the stairs, past the kitchen, and onto the service porch. The exit door was in flames, and Rand was struggling to release the wheels of the chair from some obstruction. Cari grasped the front of the wheels, pulling with all her strength. The wheelchair lurched forward, but still resisted. Cari staggered back.

"Go, Cari, go," Rand shouted. "I'll carry Maggie."

Cari watched him bend over and lift the frightened woman, then she turned and moved toward the doorway. Vaguely, she heard a crack of timber above the roar of the flames and glanced back. As if in slow motion, she watched with horror as a blackened, flaming board fell across Rand's shoulders.

Spinning around, she raced back onto the service porch, pushed the burning board from Rand's shoulders, and slapped down the flames from his shirt as he continued carrying Maggie from the burning porch.

Outside, firemen moved hoses forward and people back, and the smell of smoke filled the air. Cari was aware a fireman had left the group and hurried to help Rand. Together, they carried Maggie away from the activity. Cari followed, bending to speak to Maggie, to allow her eyes to rove over her briefly, searching for burned skin. But Maggie seemed to have escaped the flames of the falling timber.

A new wail, the familiar sound of the ambulance, sounded above the noise around the house. Cari straightened and looked at Rand. But he'd lifted his gaze from Maggie and was now scanning the crowd of people. His search stopped when he saw Jolene and Joey, and he strode across the chaotic scene to stop before them. Cari put her hand on Maggie's arm, speaking to her in a soothing voice, but her mind was on Rand. He hadn't spoken to her since he'd told her to leave the house. He'd paid no heed to the burning timber or his flaming shirt or her hands pressing the fire from the cloth. She looked down at her hands, conscious now of the pain throbbing through them. She lifted the one from Maggie's arm and stared at it in the faint light. She couldn't see the red that she knew must cover the skin.

She drew back, allowing the paramedics to care for Maggie. She pointed to Rand, saying he had been injured, and watched a paramedic approach the surgeon. She could see Rand objecting, and breathed a sigh of relief when he finally followed the medic to the ambulance.

She stayed until John arrived and she'd sent him to the hospital. She stayed until Jolene and Joey had left with Jolene's parents. She ignored her throbbing hands, thinking instead of the damage her stubbornness had caused. She knew Hawthorne House continually needed some kind of repair. Stubbornly, she'd thought if she supplied money and John repaired, everything would be all right. But everything wasn't all right. She'd refused to sell the aging house and now, people she loved had been hurt.

She stayed until only one fire truck and a few firemen remained to keep watch for any surviving embers. She looked at her hands, knowing she could not drive to the emergency room. Then a fireman approached, asking her if she had a place to stay for the night, offering to call someone. Hating her dependence, she held up her injured hands. ''A ride to the hospital.''

Chapter Twelve

"You can't go back to your house," Reba said. She drew back the thin curtain shielding Cari from the rest of the emergency room.

Cari looked at her bandaged hands ruefully. "I can't drive back, that's for sure."

"I meant come home with me."

Cari laughed weakly. "It's nice to know I don't have to sleep on a cardboard box under a bridge tonight."

"You may prefer the box after you've spent a night on my sofa."

Cari hesitated. Where she slept tonight wasn't uppermost in her mind, but she'd asked about Rand so often, she sounded like an echo. Her last inquiry had elicited the information that he'd suffered second- and third-degree burns on his back and had been admitted to the burn unit. With an effort, she refrained from asking again.

"I need to see about John and Maggie. . . ."

Reba slung her purse over her shoulder. "They're okay. The Greens came to pick them up. Oh, yes, one of the firemen came by while you were getting your hands bandaged. Said they suspect the fire was started by frayed electrical wiring or possibly a power overload. He said it's not unusual in old houses.''

Cari's heart sank. Frayed electrical wiring or power overload. She thought of John's work on the lights for the patio and Joey's father's stereo hookup. She breathed wearily. She'd tried so hard to keep up with the continuing need for repairs. She'd thought she could save Hawthorne House from demolition, and she'd lost it to fire. Why had she been so stubborn? If she'd sold the house, at least the lives of those she cared for wouldn't have been threatened. Morosely, she sat up on the gurney and slid her feet down until they touched a step stool. She glanced at Reba. ''If the doctor is through with me, we should go. You have to be in the OR in less than four hours. Which means you might get two hours' sleep.''

Reba laughed. ''We've gotten by on less.'' She held up a finger in a waiting gesture. ''Let me check with the nurse. It's probably the paperwork—which, as you know, takes longer than the treatment.''

Reba returned moments later, waving a small square of paper. ''Prescription for pain pills. Otherwise, you're outta here.''

Cari concentrated on placing one foot on the stool beside the gurney, grateful that Reba didn't spring forward and grasp her arm to assist her. Proving that she could still stand was somehow important—a small show of dignity. She'd lost enough today. Worst of all, she'd lost Rand. How could he love a woman whose stubborn, one-track mind had caused the pain he'd suffer from his burns and cause him to lose weeks or months of work? How could he ever want to see her again?

Still, she couldn't leave without seeing him. She touched Reba's hand with her gauze-covered hands. ''Would you mind if we dashed up to see Rand?''

Reba turned toward the elevator without comment, and Cari felt a flush of gratitude—and wondered if this was how wives and husbands felt when they had to assure themselves a dear one was breathing.

''He's sleeping.''

Cari gazed at the young nurse, thinking that she didn't look old enough to have graduated from high school, let alone be responsible for someone she loved.

The nurse excused herself and turned to answer an approaching physician, and Cari stood forlornly by the nurses' station. Love, she repeated silently. She loved Rand. Why hadn't she told him? She'd known it before the fire. But he'd left the hospital before she had. And then the fire . . . It was too late to tell him now. She'd almost cost him his life. She'd certainly cost him a slice out of his medical practice.

Vaguely, she saw the physician nod to the nurse and carry a patient chart to an unoccupied section of the nurses' station.

The nurse walked away from the doctor and returned her attention to Cari. ''The pain medicine Dr. Carson received in the emergency room wore off and I sedated him a few minutes ago, so I don't think it's best to wake him.''

Cari grimaced without rancor.

The nurse smiled sympathetically. ''I'll tell him you were here.''

Cari controlled the urge to bypass the nurse and assure herself Rand was breathing. Instead, she managed a civil ''thank you'' and left with Reba. At the exit, she paused. ''I forgot to tell the night supervisor I wouldn't be in to work tomorrow. That is, today.''

''I think she knows. She's the one who called to tell me you were in the ER.''

At Reba's car, Reba opened the door and helped Cari inside. Closing the door, she walked around and slid under the steering wheel.

''I know you need sleep, but would you mind driving by Hawthorne House?'' She couldn't bear to add ''to see if the fire restarted.''

Reba started the engine. ''Of course I wouldn't mind.''

''You did say John and Maggie are staying with the Greens.'' Worry laced her voice.

''I did,'' Reba said. ''Maggie didn't have one burn. Jolene and Joey are okay. And you know they went home with relatives.''

''Relatives are a nice thing to have,'' Cari said. ''And friends.'' Her voice quavered. She reached a bandaged hand toward Reba's arm, but she didn't touch it.

''You should call your mother in the morning.'' Reba turned the steering wheel and left the parking lot.

''I wouldn't know where to call her in the first place. In the second place, what could she do?''

''Not worry, for one. What if she heard from someone about the house burning?'' She turned onto Oak Street.

''That's unlikely.''

''Your aunt. Your cousin. A neighbor.''

''Mother isn't friendly with my aunt.''

''I think you should let your mother know anyway.

You could call the club where your stepfather is playing, couldn't you? Leave a message and my number.''
She drove silently until she stopped the car, and the
odor of wet, burnt timber wafted through the open
window.

Cari avoided looking at the house as they parked.
Allowing Reba to help her out of the car, she walked
to the sidewalk, raising her eyes to look at the damaged structure. To her surprise, in the faint light from
the street lamp, the front of the house looked the same.

Reba paused beside her. ''The fireman said the
damage was limited to the back porch. He said it was
difficult to believe.''

''The rest of the house is all right?''

''Smoke damaged. The fireman said they would
check in at intervals. Embers might spark again.''

Cari took a deep breath and, despite the strong odor
of wet and burnt wood, felt a sense of relief. Hawthorne House was still hers. She turned to Reba with
a weak smile. ''We might as well see if you can get
a couple of hours' sleep. That is, if you don't want to
call in and take the day off?''

Reba laughed wryly. ''With you off? I doubt having
two nurses off would sit too well with the supervisor.''

''Right,'' Cari said, her voice gruff with emotion.

Cari awoke at noon to the insistent ringing of the
telephone. She sat up in unfamiliar surroundings and
looked for the source of the sound. Finding the telephone on an end table, she brushed off a Post-it note
as she managed to cradle the receiver on her bandaged
left hand. She bent to read the note and voiced a sleepy
''hello.''

''Cari.'' Her mother's voice came over the receiver. ''I received a message for me to call you.''

Cari looked up from the note. ''Reba called. She left me a note saying she'd left a message for you before she left for work.''

''Why would Reba call? Are you okay? Is something wrong?''

''I'm fine.'' She felt an unusual sense of comfort at the concern in her mother's voice. ''We had a little fire at the house last night.''

''Were you home? Were you hurt?''

''A few burns on my hands. Which means I'm going to get a vacation whether I want it or not.''

''Was anyone else hurt?''

''The doctor who lives across the hall. He was carrying Maggie outside when a burning shelf, or something, fell on his back. He was admitted to the hospital.''

''I hope he isn't seriously injured.''

''I hope so too. I'll call the nurses' station this morning and find out his condition. If I can punch in the number,'' she added. She shifted the receiver in her left hand gingerly.

''It doesn't sound like you can move back into your house right away. And you're off work. So I have an idea.'' Cari's mother paused. ''I was going to call you anyway to ask you to come up for a weekend. Now you can stay longer.''

''I can't afford a hotel room.''

''You don't have to afford a hotel room. We have a guest room,'' her mother chortled.

''A guest room? Have you bought a house?''

''Not exactly. We bought a motor home. A mini–

motor home. And the guest room is a canopy fastened to the coach, but it's enclosed with cloth sides. I've already bought a fold-up bed because I'd planned for you to visit.''

Cari managed to keep the surprise from her voice. ''It is a good idea. I know Reba will insist I stay with her, but I'd feel like such a burden.''

''Then come and stay with us. I'm bored staying in this trailer park. We had to sell the car, and if I want to go somewhere, it means unhooking the water and electricity to the motor home before I can drive it. Bring your car. We can go places.''

So much for being wanted, Cari thought wryly. ''I can't drive, Mom. Both hands are burned. Could you catch a bus to Buena Vista and drive us back?''

''Of course. Is tomorrow too soon for you to leave?''

Cari's heart lurched. Leaving anytime was too soon. Leaving her home, her friends . . . Rand. Most of all, leaving Rand. She took a steadying breath. ''Tomorrow will be fine.'' She gave her mother Reba's address.

She'd have time to call the realtor and tell him she was willing to sell. She'd decided that was her only alternative, in the early hours of the morning when she couldn't sleep. She'd tell the realtor she'd keep in touch with her cousin to sign the necessary papers when the sale was ready to go through escrow. Then she and her mother could pack what she could take with her and make arrangements to store any furniture that wasn't damaged. She'd have to call her supervisor and tell her she'd keep in touch, call Maggie and Jolene, be sure to find her insurance card and take it with her, and convince Reba that leaving to stay with her mother was the best idea.

But first, she had to see Rand.

He was awake, but drowsy. Which was best, Cari thought, the ache in her chest heavy as she looked at him. She couldn't bear to see his eyes alert and accusing.

"Hi." She glanced down to see that the lacy shawl she wore covered her bandaged hands. "Are the nurses being good to you?"

He grinned drowsily. "I'm smothered in TLC."

She managed a chuckle. "Be sure you put that on the hospital questionnaire when you fill it out."

A semblance of his former grin touched his lips. "I will." His eyes turned toward her. "Are you all right?"

"I'm fine. And so are Jolene and Joey and John and Maggie. They've gone to stay with friends and relatives."

"What about you?"

"I'm staying with Reba until my mother comes. She's asked me to visit for a little while."

"That's nice," Rand said drowsily. "Is the house badly damaged?'

"The back porch is history."

"I'm sorry," Rand said. "But maybe you can rebuild."

"I don't think so," Cari said. "In fact, being a landlord isn't all that great. If you still want to buy, it's on the market as of today."

For a long moment, Rand didn't answer, and Cari thought he'd fallen asleep. Which was just as well. She couldn't bear to say good-bye.

She turned to leave, but his voice stopped her.

"Cari, are you sure? Jim would hate me for this, but could you rebuild?"

Cari's chest hurt, as if tears welled inside her heart. "Rebuild an aging house that could have killed you? Oh, Rand, I'm sorry, so sorry." She caught her chaotic voice. "Rebuilding is not a good idea," she said in a barely controlled voice. "Besides, I thought about moving into a condo where all I have to do when something needs fixing is call the maintenance office." Cari looked aside as a nurse, carrying a medicine tray, approached. "Looks like I've worn out my welcome," she said lightly. "You know how nurses hate to have their routines interrupted. So be good, and I'll, uh . . ." The lump in her throat appeared without warning. "I'll see you around," she said lamely.

The area surrounding Tahoe was more beautiful than Cari had imagined. Towering trees surrounded a sun-speckled lake, and the space where the motor home was parked had a stunning view. Cari's hands had been rebandaged, separating the fingers and leaving her less injured thumbs free. She'd even covered her hands with plastic and walked across the trailer park to the showers.

During the next week, she called Reba four times, chatting about the scenery and the casinos and asking about the operating room and Reba's romance, when all she wanted to talk about was Rand. She didn't. She only asked about his recovery as casually as possible and repressed the swell of her heart when Reba added "He asks about you."

With a barely legible scrawl, in the presence of a

notary, she signed the papers to sell the house and returned them. She and her mother went sightseeing or window-shopping daily, ambled through the casinos, and went to hear the band play in the evening. But none of the activities kept her from thinking of Rand.

At the end of three weeks, she knew she could not return to Buena Vista.

She cradled the telephone in her healing hands. ''Reba, I wanted to tell you before I called the supervisor. I'm resigning from Buena Vista.'' She hurried her words over Reba's protest. ''When Mom leaves, I'll rent a room and work for the nursing registry. You'll have to come and visit me. Tahoe is beautiful.''

With her hands healed and her parents gone, she asked for as much time as possible with the registry. With the sale of the house, she didn't need the extra money, but she hated to be in her room alone. She couldn't keep thoughts of Rand at bay.

She drove back to Buena Vista once to meet with the realtor and open a long-term savings account. She told herself she should move the account to Tahoe, but somehow, she couldn't break her last tie to Buena Vista. Nor could she keep herself from driving by the site of Hawthorne House.

The ground was bare. Not a plank from the flooring or a gingerbread carving littered the scraped, denuded soil. Only a bulldozer hovered over the site. Cari drove past without stopping.

In August, she called Reba and asked her to visit for the weekend. ''Only if we can talk about wedding plans,'' Reba chortled. ''Of course, you'll be my maid of honor,'' she added between her exultant additions to her announcement.

Cari agreed with mixed feelings. Would Rand be there? Reba had mentioned inviting the people who worked in the operating room and some of the doctors and their wives or fiancées. She hadn't mentioned Rand since she'd told her he had returned to work. Maybe he had married, maybe he had a fiancée. Cari couldn't bear to ask. How could she go back and see Rand and find another woman holding his arm? But how could she refuse to be the maid of honor at her best friend's wedding?

Cari returned to Buena Vista in late September for Reba's wedding. She avoided Oak Street on her way to Reba's apartment. Amid the cheerful chaos, she donned a pale peach, ankle-length dress and a lacy, wide-brimmed matching hat.

Arriving at the church, one of the ushers, a scrub tech from the operating room, showed her the room where the other members of the wedding party had gathered. Before leaving her, he eyed her mischievously. ''Didn't you know you're not supposed to look prettier than the bride, Cari?'' He winked. ''I'll catch you later. Save me all your dances.''

Cari managed a smile and hurried inside.

The bride was calm and lovely in a floor-length, antique white wedding dress. The groom was nervous and handsome in a pale blue tuxedo. And the wedding ceremony was a beautiful blur to Cari.

She stayed at the church for pictures with the wedding party and didn't see Rand until she reached the reception hall.

Her heart flip-flopped when she saw him at the buffet table. An attractive, green-eyed, dark-haired woman in a pale green dress chatted with him, and Cari could hear his familiar laughter. An ache touched her heart as he carried the woman's plate to a distant table.

He remained standing after the woman was seated, his gaze roaming the room restlessly. Then his eyes stopped and he was staring at Cari. She felt immobilized.

She saw him bend over and speak to his companion, and then he weaved through the throng of guests toward Cari.

''Cari, it's good to see you.''

''It's good to see you too,'' Cari said inanely. Her heart was throbbing overtime all the way to her toes, and she wanted to touch him. But she couldn't move, and apparently she couldn't speak. No words came to mind.

''How are the hands? Any scars?'' He reached forward and took her hands in his, turning them over to look at the palms. With one finger, he gently touched a large, pale area in the center of one palm. ''One, I see.'' He looked up without releasing her hands. ''I was a little foggy the last time I saw you. Did I thank you for saving my skin from total destruction?''

''How is your back?'' Cari asked. *How is your life? Do you sleep well at night? Do you ever think of me? Do you miss me like I miss you?*

''Healed well, I'm told. If there's any scarring, I've been too busy this summer to show it off at the swimming pool.''

I know. Building the clinic. Dating dark-haired

beauties. "You must have rented one of those fancy condos."

"Not quite. But there is a pool." He released her hands. "Can I get you something to eat?" He motioned toward the laden buffet tables.

Still worrying about my nutrition. A fleeting thought of the late-night dinner in her apartment made Cari's heart flop again. "I don't think so. It's been a hectic day. My stomach hasn't settled down yet."

"Maybe a drive in the fresh air will help?"

"I shouldn't leave."

"Just a little while wouldn't be noticed. I'll make it a short drive."

Cari shook her head. A short drive to show her his new clinic. She didn't need salt in her wounds.

"Please?" Rand tilted his head endearingly, and Cari laughed softly. Through a break in the crowd, she saw the friendly usher–surgical tech working his way toward her.

"You win. Is there a side door?"

"I'll find one."

At the intersection, Rand turned toward the main highway instead of Oak Street. He made a turn onto a two-lane road, and then another on an even less traveled road. Giant oak trees shaded uneven pastures. Houses, some with large barns, appeared at intervals. Cari made no comment until he had been driving for ten minutes or so. "Is this the long way to somewhere?"

"We'll reach our destination in about five minutes," Rand said cheerfully. "Something I want you to see." He turned onto what appeared to be more a lane than a road. Olive trees, their silvery leaves catching the late sunlight, bordered each side.

Cari sighed. At least it wouldn't be the clinic. The scenery was lovely and could certainly be calming to a distraught patient. But Rand would have to provide road maps to find the place. Cari smiled contentedly. It was a nice drive. The lane and the trees and the sunlit silence seemed to go on forever.

Without warning, Rand slowed the car, made a left turn, and stopped with the car facing a structure. Cari gasped. Framed by the windshield, spotlighted in a pool of sunlight, Hawthorne House preened like a celebrity awaiting the flash of a camera light.

She turned to gaze at Rand in bewilderment. He gave her a small, satisfied grin, slid from behind the steering wheel, and walked around to open the car door for her.

''Want to take a closer look?''

Cari followed him in a wonderful daze. ''How . . .'' She couldn't find the words to continue.

Rand laughed. ''Moving companies are miracle workers—for a price.''

Cari bounded up the steps and stopped at the door in new wonder. ''The stained glass is still intact.''

She looked at Rand, questions darkening her eyes. ''How?'' she repeated.

''One of the doctors on the Buena Vista staff bought the land, but his wife didn't want to build this far from the city. So he sold it to me with no down payment. Since I owned the house, all I had to do was come up with the money for the movers. Simple.''

Cari's throat swelled and tears ached behind her eyes. He hadn't torn down Hawthorne House.

''The nice part is,'' Rand continued, ''I'm willing to sell to the right buyer. No down payment. Just what I owe on the land.'' He looked at Cari, uncertainty, and maybe longing, filling his eyes.

Cari looked away. She felt a warm tear rise and fall over the rim of her eye. The house was hers, but she knew now the house was not what she wanted. Without Rand to share it with her, it was no longer important.

''Would you be interested in that kind of deal?''

Cari could hear the strain behind Rand's forced levity. She swallowed. She wanted to tell him the only deal she was interested in was spending the rest of her life with him. But that was only a fantasy. Her family didn't spend the rest of their lives with their spouses.

''Cari.'' Rand grasped Cari's shoulders and turned her to face him. ''It isn't the house I'm offering you. It's me. I love you.'' His voice broke. ''I know you find it hard to forgive me for buying your house, but I didn't wreck it. It's still a marvelous old house. It still holds memories, and we could make so many more together.''

''I'm not good marriage material,'' Cari said, her gaze unable to leave his eyes.

''Practice makes perfect.'' Hope glimmered in Rand's eyes.

''My mother is still practicing and she hasn't got it right yet.''

''Maybe she didn't have the right teacher.''

''Do you think that makes a difference?'' The lilt in Cari's heart carried to her voice.

''Oh, definitely.'' Rand aped the lilt in Cari's voice.

Cari closed her eyes, unable to bear the surge of

hope welling in her chest. Did she dare take a chance? She thought of Reba, who had no problem with promising to keep her wedding vows. Cari felt her heart tremble. Her family wasn't like Reba's. ''My family isn't known for successful marriages.''

''We could start a new family tradition.'' Rand's voice was filled with emotion.

Cari gazed into Rand's warm, dark eyes. ''I'd like that,'' she said softly. She lifted her arms and curved them around his neck and pulled his head down. ''I love you.''

He lowered his head and his lips covered hers, and she felt as if sunlight danced in her head. She felt gay and light-headed and loved. When he finally pulled away, he glanced at the house and then smiled back at her. ''Do I get a vote on remodeling the kitchen?''

A small oriole sailed through the air and landed on an olive branch, making his arrival known with a melodic chirp. ''And the nursery and the bedroom and the rose garden.''

Rand brushed her lips lightly. ''I do have a medical practice,'' he murmured.

And a new clinic. And I have to apply for an operating position at Beuna Vista. Cari sighed, tangling her fingers in the hair at the nape of his neck. ''We'll work around that.''

She lifted her lips, and he lowered his head and covered her mouth with his. The small bird in the olive tree broke into song.